"You gave a child up for adoption, right?"

For the breath of an instant, Rebecca's heart stopped beating. No one, not even her closest friends, knew about the decision that had been made years ago. How could this man, a total stranger—

"My name is Sam Winslow. I adopted a child fourteen years ago."

Breathe. Just breathe. This couldn't be happening. Rebecca waited in vain for the rapid cadence of her heart to slow, but the pounding continued.

"I petitioned the court to open her adoption records. You're listed as my daughter's birth mother."

His words penetrated the fog surrounding her, and she looked at him. A daughter! She had a daughter. She hadn't even known whether the child had been a boy or a girl.

The room spun. Rebecca clutched the edge of the desk to steady herself. She'd prayed, hoped and dreamed that her child would one day want to meet her. Were her dreams finally coming true?

Dear Reader,

Welcome to Harlequin American Romance. With your search for satisfying reading in mind, every month Harlequin American Romance aims to offer you a stimulating blend of heartwarming, emotional and deeply romantic stories.

Unexpected arrivals lead to the sweetest of surprises as Harlequin American Romance celebrates the love only a baby can bring, in our brand-new promotion, AMERICAN BABY, which begins this month with Jacqueline Diamond's delightful *Surprise, Doc! You're a Daddy!* After months of searching for her missing husband, Meg Avery finally finds him—only, Dr. Hugh Menton doesn't remember her or their child!

With Valor and Devotion, the latest book in Charlotte Maclay's exciting MEN OF STATION SIX series, is a must-read about a valorous firefighter who rescues an orphaned boy. Will the steadfast bachelor consider becoming a devoted family man after meeting the little boy's pretty social worker? JUST FOR KIDS, Mary Anne Wilson's new miniseries, debuts with *Regarding the Tycoon's Toddler....* This trilogy focuses on a corporate day-care center and the lives and loves of those who work there. And don't miss *The Biological Bond* by Jamie Denton, the dramatic story of a mother who is reunited with the child she'd been forced to give away, when her daughter's adoptive single father seeks her help.

Enjoy this month's offerings, and be sure to return each and every month to Harlequin American Romance!

Wishing you happy reading,

Melissa Jeglinski
Associate Senior Editor
Harlequin American Romance

THE BIOLOGICAL BOND

Jamie Denton

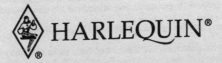

TORONTO • NEW YORK • LONDON
AMSTERDAM • PARIS • SYDNEY • HAMBURG
STOCKHOLM • ATHENS • TOKYO • MILAN • MADRID
PRAGUE • WARSAW • BUDAPEST • AUCKLAND

This book can only be dedicated to two very special women...
To Joan—For having the courage to make the tough choices;
and
To Alice—For taking a child into her heart
and making that child her own.
I love you both.

ISBN 0-373-16892-6

THE BIOLOGICAL BOND

Copyright © 2001 by Jamie Ann Denton.

Visit us at www.eHarlequin.com

Printed in U.S.A.

ABOUT THE AUTHOR

Ever since she heard her first fairy tale, award-winning Harlequin author Jamie Denton always believed in happily-ever-after and the power of love. In her opinion, there's nothing quite as heartwarming as the happy ending for a hero and heroine who overcome the odds. Always one to seek out a challenge, Jamie embraced her first challenge at the age of sixteen when she married her high school sweetheart. A whole lot of years later, she still fondly recalls the first time she saw her own personal hero and knew, even at that tender age, that he was the one for her. With a history like that, what else could she write except romances?

Books by Jamie Denton

HARLEQUIN AMERICAN ROMANCE

892—THE BIOLOGICAL BOND

Dear Reader,

I've always been one to look for challenges and have always enjoyed tackling them. Writing *The Biological Bond* was one such challenge, and one that was close to my own heart for a number of reasons. For as long as I can remember, I knew I was adopted. Even though I grew up with this knowledge and never had a single moment of doubt about the love of my adoptive parents, it didn't stop me from embarking upon the same fantasies that nearly every adopted child has about their biological parents. At the age of nineteen, the opportunity arose and I was able to live out that fantasy by locating my birth mother. Not only am I blessed with parents who love me, but I also have a whole new family to share in my life.

The Biological Bond is an exploration of the emotional upheaval experienced by the biological and adoptive parents of a young girl in need of a life-saving procedure, a procedure that only the birth parent can provide. To further complicate matters, there is the undeniable attraction between birth and biological parent. And of course, there is the secret of the child's parentage and what could happen if the truth was ever revealed.

I hope you enjoy your time with Sam and Rebecca as much as I did. I'd love to hear what you think. Write to me at P.O. Box 224, Mohall, North Dakota 58761-0224, e-mail to jamie@jamiedenton.net or visit my Web site at www.jamiedenton.net

Sincerely,

Jamie Denton

Prologue

"We've found her, Mr. Winslow. She's in Los Angeles, California. Would you like us to make initial contact?"

Sam Winslow, Jr., glanced again at the photograph of Rebecca Martinson. Familiar green eyes gazed at him, and his hand shook. He wondered how she could she have done it. And why? He'd never understood the inner workings of a woman's mind, but this particular woman he *needed* to understand.

"No," Sam said, dropping the photo on the investigator's desk. "I'll leave for L.A. in the morning. I can handle things from here."

Sam stood. If he was going to catch the morning flight for California, he had plenty to take care of before he left. Picking up the photograph again, he slipped it into the thick manila envelope the investigator provided.

Details.

Details of Rebecca Martinson.

For a woman who didn't want to be found, she'd been relatively simple to locate.

He extended his hand to the investigator and thanked him before leaving the office. Tucking the envelope under his arm, he headed toward his pickup, slipped inside and tossed the offending material on the seat.

He wasn't looking forward to this trip. Hell, he wasn't looking forward to meeting *her*. And he wouldn't have bothered, if he hadn't needed her to save his daughter's life.

Chapter One

"There's a Mr. Winslow here to see you, Rebecca."

Rebecca Martinson set aside the file she'd spent the morning reading and looked at her secretary. "A new case?" she asked Laura, wondering whatever happened to marriages that lasted forever. As a family law attorney, she'd seen the uglier side of marriage and, in some instances, humanity as well. She knew from her myriad of clients that happily-ever-after was nothing more than fodder for fairy tales. The only bright spots in her chosen profession were the adoptions she handled. Nothing could compare to the happiness on the faces of the adoptive couples or the love they gave to the child who'd been chosen. Her adoption cases gave her hope.

"He won't say, and he doesn't have an appointment." Laura wiggled her eyebrows. "But he's the most drop-dead-gorgeous specimen I've seen around here in ages."

Rebecca smiled. "I've got a few minutes before

the staff meeting. I'll see what he wants, then you can get started on whatever paperwork we might need."

Laura nodded, opened the door, and Mr. Winslow walked into the office. For once her secretary hadn't exaggerated. This man was truly a sight to behold. He had "cowboy" written all over him, and Rebecca's insides fluttered. Rough-hewn features and broad shoulders teased her feminine senses. She glanced away. She hadn't been that affected by the male species since...well, in a very long time.

"Would you like some coffee, Mr. Winslow?" Laura asked.

"No, thank you." His deep voice commanded attention, not to mention the jeans that emphasized long legs and strong thighs. He had the kind of well-tuned body Rebecca appreciated just a little too much.

Forcing her mind on business, she rounded the desk and extended her hand. His rough, callused hand clasped hers firmly. This was a man who worked with his hands for a living, she thought. Powerful hands.

"I'm Rebecca Martinson, Mr. Winslow." She motioned to a chair. "Won't you sit down?"

He nodded, then crossed the office and sat in the chair opposite her desk. A deep-brown corduroy jacket, complete with elbow patches, matched the color of his hair—a tad too long for a label like *clean-cut*.

She returned to her own chair and looked at him expectantly. "What can I do for you, Mr. Winslow?"

The cowboy shifted and glanced around her office,

taking time to examine the multitude of diplomas and awards on the wall behind her desk. When his gaze fastened on her, she smiled, hoping to set him at ease.

"Why don't you start by telling me why you need a lawyer, Mr. Winslow." She pulled a legal pad from her tray and wrote his name at the top.

He cleared his throat and looked at her with deep, chocolate-colored eyes. His lips were drawn in a thin line. He looked so serious, and a little angry. Not an unusual emotion in her line of work.

She set her pen on the pad, growing a little uncomfortable under his intense scrutiny. "Mr. Winslow, the initial consultation is free, but I have to warn you, I have a full schedule today. Perhaps you'd like to do this another time when you're more comfortable—"

He leaned forward, bracing his elbows on his knees. Some emotion she couldn't define sparked his gaze. "You gave a child up for adoption, right?"

For the breath of an instant her heart stopped beating. If someone had sucker-punched her midsection, she couldn't have been more shocked. No one, not even her closest friends, knew about the decision that had been made fourteen years ago. How could this man, a total stranger...

"Who are you?" she demanded, rising.

"My name is Sam Winslow. I adopted a child fourteen years ago."

Breathe. Just breathe.

This couldn't be happening, she thought, sucking vital air into her lungs. She waited in vain for the rapid cadence of her heart to slow, but the pounding continued.

I adopted a child fourteen years ago.

Maybe it was a coincidence.

I adopted a child fourteen years ago.

There was no other explanation. There *could* be no other explanation. Hadn't her father seen to it that no one would ever learn the truth?

"My daughter has a condition called aplastic anemia," Sam Winslow continued in a matter-of-fact tone as if he hadn't just tipped her world upside down. "If she doesn't have a bone-marrow transplant, she'll die. We haven't been able to find a match, so I petitioned the court to open her adoption records. You're listed as her birth mother."

The room spun. Rebecca clutched the edge of the desk to steady herself. She'd prayed, hoped and dreamed that her child would one day want to meet her. At odd times she'd find herself wondering whether if things had been different she could have kept her child. Only things hadn't been different, they'd been impossible.

Mr. Winslow's words penetrated the fog surrounding her, and she looked at him. A daughter! She had a daughter. She hadn't even known whether the child had been a boy or a girl—until now. She'd given birth, and the nurses had whisked the baby away, but not before she'd heard that first cry of life. A sound that had been haunting her dreams for fourteen long years.

Now that child could very well die. Her heart broke all over again.

"I...I have a...a daughter?" she whispered, still reeling from Sam Winslow's claim.

His expression tightened and he stood. "No, Ms. Martinson. *I* have a daughter."

The truth stung and scraped along her raw emotions. He was absolutely right. She didn't have a daughter. He did. Legally. Emotionally was an altogether different scenario.

And it did nothing to stop the myriad of questions swimming through her mind. From the sharp tone of his voice, she had a feeling Winslow wouldn't be forthcoming with answers. "What's her name?"

He shoved his hands deep in his pockets. "I don't believe that's relevant."

Sam turned and strode to the window overlooking Wilshire Boulevard, fifteen floors below. He never cared much for big cities, especially ones like Los Angeles with its smog, crime and overcrowded conditions. Previous experience reminded him that a twenty-mile drive could take more than an hour during rush hour. Wide-open spaces and untamed land, land that provided for his family, were more his speed.

He shouldn't have come here, but he'd run out of options. Mel needed this woman to save her life. He was completely helpless, and he hated the feeling. And the way Rebecca Martinson looked at him, with those damn big green eyes of hers, made him uncomfortable as hell. Eyes just like—

"Mel," he said.

He didn't know why he'd enlightened her, but the vulnerability and pain he'd detected in her eyes tugged at him. What harm was there in her knowing his daughter's name?

"Mel? You named a girl Mel?"

She sounded like Christina, his ex-wife, and he bristled. Christina had despised it when he'd called their adorable dark-haired, green-eyed little girl Mel. Undignified, she'd called it. "It's short for Melanie."

Silence stretched between them. He wanted to leave, to hop on a plane and fly home where he belonged. But Mel needed this woman—her birth mother.

"How do you know I'll be a compatible match?" Her voice sounded faraway, dream-like. But this wasn't a dream—it was a nightmare—*his* nightmare.

He spun around to face her. "We don't," he stated. "The test is simple, and once it's determined you're a match, you can donate the bone marrow. I'm told the removal is a relatively simple procedure—"

"I know how it works, Mr. Winslow," she snapped.

"Good. Then you agree?"

She stared at him, her eyes pooling with unshed tears. He didn't want to see her tears. He didn't want to care that she cried. All he wanted was to know that she was willing to save his daughter's life.

"I need an answer, Ms. Martinson."

She gave him a watery smile. "Call me Rebecca."

"I need an answer, *Ms. Martinson*." There'd be no Rebecca or Sam for them. If she was a match, she'd donate the marrow, then be out of their lives as if she'd never existed. Mel wouldn't even have to know who had donated the marrow. "I've already made arrangements to have you tested as soon as possible. Today."

She stared at him in stunned silence.

"To make this as simple as possible, I'll have a phlebotomist come to your office," he told her. "We can have the results in a few hours. I'll call you as soon as we know something. When's the best time?"

He didn't know if she was going to deny him or not and decided not to take any chances. He had no trouble playing dirty if it meant saving Mel. He'd do whatever was necessary if it meant saving his daughter's life, even asking the court for an order to force Mel's birth mother to give his daughter what she needed.

He moved closer to the desk, braced his hands on the polished surface and leaned forward. "Ms. Martinson, my daughter could die. She needs your help. You *gave* her life," he said, going for the kill. "A blood test could be all it takes to *save* her life."

She bit her lip, and those eyes that reminded him too much of his daughter filled with emotion. "I have a staff meeting in a few minutes, then I have to be in court this afternoon. I can always get someone to cover for me.'' Her long, slender fingers trembled as she lifted her hand to rub at her temple. "Whenever you can arrange it is fine.''

He calmly handed her a card indicating the name of the lab he'd made prior arrangements with before coming to see her. It had been a gamble, but he was past the point of playing it safe. He'd wanted all avenues covered before he'd approached her and was pleased that his instincts had paid off.

He moved toward the door, relieved the first step had been accomplished. In a matter of hours he'd have his answer.

"Wait!'' she called as he reached for the door. "What happens if I'm a match?''

"Then you'll need to check into a hospital to have the bone marrow extracted.''

Anxious to put some distance between himself and Rebecca Martinson, he reached for the door handle again.

"Wait!''

He glanced over his shoulder at her.

"Is she going to be all right? Will a transplant work?''

Her soft voice held a plea that touched his heart. "I hope so, Ms. Martinson.''

He opened the door and looked back at her one last time. He'd always wondered where Mel had gotten those big green eyes and raven's wing hair. Now he knew.

She looked as if she wanted to say something. Sam

didn't want to hear it. "I'll be in touch," he said. As he strode out of the elegant law office, he wondered why he wasn't relieved.

REBECCA TRIED TO CONCENTRATE, but no matter how hard she attempted to focus on the cases the associates who reported to her had prepared to discuss at the weekly staff meeting, the more her mind drifted to her daughter and Sam Winslow. Now that she'd gotten over her initial shock, she had questions. Simple questions, silly ones really, like what her daughter looked like, whether or not she liked chocolate ice cream topped with fresh strawberries, a daily staple during her pregnancy. Did Mel wrinkle her nose at the sight of meat loaf? Did she like to read? Was she a math whiz? Did she have a desire to practice law like the rest of the Martinsons, or maybe she dreamed of studying medicine like her mother's side of the family?

There were more questions, tougher ones she had no answers for and was even afraid to ask...like, did her daughter want to meet the woman who had been forced to give her up for adoption?

"Rebecca?"

She let out a frustrated breath and turned her attention to Jillian Thatcher, the newest associate in the family law department. "I'm sorry, you were saying?"

"The Templeton adoption," Jillian said, opening

the file on her lap. "I was wondering if you were going to cover the bench trial."

Rebecca sat up straight and tapped her index finger against her lips. There was a chance her client, Peter Grant, could lose his parental rights, which was a subject close to her own heart. His ex-wife had remarried, moved to South Carolina with her new husband, and had been difficult at best when it came to her client's visitation. The former Mrs. Grant was alleging her ex-husband hadn't exercised his parental rights in five years. This was a tough case, and one she didn't feel the new associate was prepared to handle alone. And one that Rebecca wanted to win, not only for her client, but for herself, as well.

"When is the trial scheduled?" she asked, an idea skirting around the fringes of her mind. A dangerous idea with a steep price tag.

Jillian flipped through the file. "Two months. We have most of the pretrial discovery completed."

Rebecca nodded. Two months would allow her to see the plan forming executed. "What about phone bills? Do we have them yet?"

"Not yet."

"Get them," Rebecca instructed. "We can use them as evidence that our client has attempted to maintain contact with his children. Also get in touch with the child support unit in the County Clerk's Office. I want verification of all his support payments over the last ten years. Subpoena the clerk into trial if you have to. You'll be second chairing this one."

Jillian smiled, the excitement of stepping into a courtroom for an actual trial evident. She nodded, then jotted notes on a legal pad.

Rebecca checked her watch. If she closed the meeting now she might be able to catch Victor Furnari before he scooted out of the office for his standard two-hour lunch with the other senior partners. She needed her head examined for what she was considering.

"Is there anything else?" she asked, scanning the group.

When no one spoke, she stood and scooped a sheaf of papers into her out box. The associates took the action as a signal for the end of their meeting and gathered their files.

"I wanted to discuss the settlement conference on the Barker divorce." Lee, the more senior of the associates, was close to becoming a junior partner. She liked him. He was ambitious and smart. He could be sympathetic or brutal in the courtroom, a skill that afforded him an excellent track record.

"Can it wait until tomorrow, Lee?" she asked, rounding her desk and heading for the door.

"Sure," he said, following her. "We don't go before Judge Holden for another week."

"Check with Laura," she said, closing her office door. "Tell her I said to squeeze you in tomorrow."

She dropped a file on Laura's desk, then went directly to the elevators that would take her up to the offices of the senior partners. She stepped off the el-

evator into the plush reception area with its soft gray
carpeting and elegant furnishings. Understated art-
work adorned rich mahogany-paneled walls. She nodded a greeting to the receptionist and turned left toward Victor Furnari's office.

She approached the open door and peered inside.
Victor stood before a miniconference table, a mug of
coffee in his hand as he examined a variety of photographs. "Victor?" she called softly, not wanting to
startle him.

He turned and smiled at the sound of her voice.
"Come in, Rebecca. I was just trying to decide which
of these would best sway the court into believing my
client's husband is hiding assets. What do you think?
This thirty-thousand-dollar piece of horse flesh he
'gifted' his brother, or this receipt for a little five-
carat bauble the tabloids reported he gave to his leading lady last week."

She stepped into the office that had more mascu-
linely elegant furnishings. "Why not both?" she suggested, coming to stand next to her boss.

"Because?" Victor challenged, indicating a chair
at the table.

"Simple," she said and sat. "I would attempt to
establish Cristina Howard as the poor wife of a phi-
landering husband." She glanced at the blowup of the
exclusive jewelry store receipt. "Go for the sympathy
angle, Victor. No matter how sexist is it, especially
since you have a woman judge. Another woman can
easily relate to a woman who's worked two jobs to

put her husband through school. I doubt that it'd matter Mr. Howard chose acting lessons over med school.''

"Good choice," Vic said, lifting his mug in salute.

When she'd first started at Denison, Ross & Furnari, Victor Furnari had been a brutal taskmaster, constantly throwing challenges in front of her. It hadn't taken long for her to prove herself, and as a result she'd been given the esteemed honor of second chairing his trials. After Victor had taken ill during a particularly difficult case, Rebecca had stepped in and won the case and many that followed, resulting in her eventual status of junior partner. She loved her job, despite her father's reference to her ambitions as wasted Martinson talent.

"So what brings you up here today?" He sat in one of the conference chairs and faced her. "Certainly not a burning desire to discuss the Howard divorce," he added with a chuckle.

She gave him a thin smile. No, her purpose for breaching the walls of Mahogany Row were much more important than the divorce of one of Hollywood's hottest actors. "I need to take a leave of absence."

His salt-and-pepper brows pulled into a curious frown. "For how long?" he asked, setting his mug on the table.

"I'm not sure," she said. She wasn't certain her outrageous plan would see fruition, but she had to try. "I was thinking four weeks."

"Four weeks?" His frown deepened when she remained silent. "Are you asking me to grant your request without asking for an explanation?"

She gave a humorless chuckle. "I had hoped."

Victor stood, crossed the room and closed the door. "You've worked for me for a long time," he said coming back to sit across from her. "You know whatever happens in this office stays in this office, but I can't go to the other partners for approval without an explanation."

This was one part of her plan she'd been dreading. There were court appearances to reschedule or shift to the associates under her supervision. She had a bench trial for support modification scheduled for next week, but she was confident Lee, or even Jillian, could handle the case without any problems. No, she dreaded telling Victor *why* she wanted, needed, the time away from work. If she were in his position, she'd definitely expect an explanation. The dread settling in the pit of her stomach stemmed from her admiration and respect for Victor Furnari. Could he understand the fear and desperation of a seventeen-year-old girl who hadn't been given a choice? Would the compassion she'd always admired be extended to her?

She stood, nervous energy making her edgy. "First of all, I'm not certain I'll need the time off," she said, and moved to the window overlooking the Los Angeles skyline. "I won't know until later today."

She turned and rested her backside against the window frame, gripping the ledge with her fingers. Victor leaned back in the chair, his elbows resting on the arm, tapping his fingers together as he waited for her to continue.

"I may be a match for a child who needs a bone marrow transplant."

Victor shrugged. "Okay, but donating marrow isn't a month-long procedure. It's not like donating a kidney, but only around a week-long recovery process at best."

"I'm aware of that. But this is more complicated." She pulled in a deep breath. "The child is my daughter."

He didn't say anything for a moment, just looked at her with shrewd hazel eyes. "I didn't know you had a child," he said carefully.

"I don't. Not legally," she said and wrapped her arms around her middle. Legalities were the least of her problems. Right now the issues plaguing her were much more emotional. "She was given up for adoption when I was seventeen. Her adoptive father came to see me about an hour ago."

She explained what little she knew about Sam Winslow and her daughter's life-threatening illness, even going so far as to share with Victor the less painful details of the events surrounding the child she'd been forced to give away. He remained silent, until she said, "I want a chance to get to know my daughter."

He stood suddenly and crossed the space separating them. Gently he laid a hand on her shoulder in a silent offer of comfort. "I've known you since you were fresh out of law school. You're a very intelligent woman, Rebecca, and an excellent attorney. I'm talking to you as a friend, not your employer. Meeting this little girl is not the move of a smart person. Don't do this."

She knew he was right. The analytical part of her understood she was courting disaster, but her heart spoke another story, even if it meant she would accomplish nothing more than a broken heart. "I have to, Victor," she said quietly.

He shoved his hands in the pockets of his trousers. "For God's sake, why?" he asked, his voice filled with frustration.

"Because I didn't have a choice. For some reason that I'm not willing to question, I've been given a chance now, and I have to take it."

"Rebecca—"

"I can't turn my back on her," she argued, before he could issue further opposition.

He sighed. "I'm not saying you have to. Do whatever is required medically, but don't go anywhere near this child. You know the risks."

True, she knew the risks, but she was willing to take them. And all she had to do was convince Sam Winslow she was entitled to at least meet the daughter she'd been forced to give away fourteen years before. "I have to, Victor. She's my daughter."

He shook his head, his gaze filled with concern. God, she thought, if only her own father had been as compassionate, she might not even be having this discussion right now.

"No, Rebecca," he said gently. "She's Winslow's daughter. And since you're determined to go through with this, then you'd better remember that."

Chapter Two

As the afternoon eased into early evening, each time the telephone on her desk rang, Rebecca jumped. The lab had sent someone within an hour of Sam's departure, and she'd been waiting for his phone call ever since. Five hours later and still no word from Sam Winslow.

She'd prayed she'd be a compatible match, but, from the Internet research she'd conducted while indulging in a microwave lunch at her desk, she knew her chances weren't all that high. A twin was the most likely, then a sibling, lastly a parent. But she could still pray, and she did.

Her research had told her a great deal about aplastic anemia as well. From what the medical journals reported, the disease was indeed as serious as Winslow indicated. Melanie, *her daughter,* could very well die. She didn't know any of the details, but it was more than likely Melanie had suffered some sort of low-grade infection that had gone untreated for the anemia to require such drastic measures. She wondered how such a thing could have happened, but she didn't want to pass judgment on anyone at this point.

The shock she'd been feeling since Sam made the purpose of his visit known had finally worn off. She'd been fighting against the tears ever since, refusing to unleash the pain and silence of the past. Once again tears burned the backs of her eyes. She wanted to give in, but she couldn't. Too many years of conditioning prevented her from releasing the pent-up emotions.

The waiting was killing her. She had a schedule to rearrange and cases to farm out if her plan worked. Since her conversation with Victor, she'd spent more than a few moments wondering if he was right. Perhaps she should just do whatever was required medically and leave well enough alone.

If only Winslow would call, she could set the wheels in motion. For a brief instant she wondered what her father would say if he knew what she had planned. She shook her head. Silence would serve as her protection against Justice Martinson's wrath. She'd made the mistake of trusting him once. This was one secret she wouldn't reveal to anyone—especially her father.

The telephone on the edge of her desk rang, and she jumped. This was it. Since returning from her court appearance earlier that afternoon, she'd instructed Laura no calls unless it was Sam Winslow.

She stared at the phone as it rang a second time. What if he didn't agree? She didn't think he would turn her down—he'd told her she was needed.

The phone rang a third time and she reached for it. "Rebecca Martinson."

"This is Sam Winslow." His deep voice filtered through the phone lines. She didn't have to see him to know his lips were probably drawn in that ever-present tight line.

"We have the results. How soon can you check into the hospital?"

Despite the hint of relief in his voice, his words were still clipped and somewhat brusque. Rebecca wondered what his reaction would be when she told him what she wanted. She didn't care what Sam Winslow thought of her. Nothing was important now except that she have the chance to save her daughter's life, and convince her daughter's father that she be allowed to spend a few days with the girl.

She took a deep breath and gathered her courage. "Mr. Winslow, I'd like to discuss this with you further. Where are you staying?"

Silence.

She bit her lip, waiting. Hoping.

After a moment he rattled off the address to his hotel, which she jotted down. She checked her watch. "I'll be there within the hour," she said, and hung up the phone.

Bracing her hands on the edge of her desk, she hung her head for a moment and said a quick prayer of thanks. She really wasn't much of a religious person, but since she'd made her decision, she'd recited every prayer she remembered.

SAM FACED THE WINDOW overlooking the rear parking lot of the hotel, waiting. He glanced at his watch again for the fifth time. She would be arriving any moment now. He scowled.

A sleek, black, foreign sports car pulled into the parking lot, and he watched its slow progress across the asphalt. Instinct told him it was her.

The car slid into the parking slot two floors below. He held his breath, a part of him hoping she wouldn't come. Seconds later she slipped from the car.

She looked cool, despite the hot August evening, her white linen suit unrumpled even in the sweltering heat. Her rich dark hair was pulled back and fancily secured so it hung halfway down her back. There was no denying where Mel's beauty came from—her birth mother.

He stepped away from the window when she turned and headed toward the luxury hotel. Rebecca Martinson may be intelligent, a hot-shot lawyer, according to the report the investigator provided him with, and beyond beautiful, but he knew her type all too well. According to the investigator, Mel's birth mother had a pedigree to rival royalty.

Rebecca Martinson's father was a State Supreme Court Justice, her grandfather had been a United States Senator, brutally assassinated. As for Mel's maternal grandmother, she was simply one more cardiologist in a long line of top medical practitioners in the country.

As painful as the subject was, he couldn't help

wondering about Mel's biological father. The investigator had been evasive in his answers on that score, and had provided nothing by way of solid information. Was Mel's natural father the son of a servant the mighty Martinson family had been ashamed of? Or was he someone high on the "A" list anxious to avoid scandal? Or was it something as simple as the fact that Rebecca hadn't been more than a child herself?

A knock on the door interrupted his train of thought. She wanted to talk. His gut said she wanted something. He could feel it just as sure as he could feel the cool breezes from the plains where he grew up, and it filled him with a deep sense of dread.

She knocked again, and he opened the door. Standing in the hallway, she was no longer the self-assured attorney he'd first glimpsed. Now she was nervous, almost as nervous as he was about this meeting.

"Hi," she said quietly when she stepped into the room.

"I'd offer you a drink, Ms. Martinson, but this isn't a social call. What do you want?"

He knew he was being hard, but dammit, he didn't like feeling threatened. And Rebecca Martinson was a threat of the worst possible kind. She didn't have a legal right to demand squat. Emotionally, well, that was an entirely different situation.

She set her purse on the cream sofa, and he couldn't help noticing how her hands trembled. She started to remove her lightweight linen blazer, then changed her mind and pulled it back around her, shoving her hands in the side pockets.

She cleared her throat, her gaze darting around the suite. He remained by the closed door and crossed his arms over his chest. He wasn't going to make this easy for her, whatever the hell it was she wanted from him.

"Mr. Winslow, I would like the chance to get to know my dau—to get to know Melanie."

Anger, pure and hot, flared through him. He should have expected something like this. His visit had more than likely stirred some dormant maternal instinct. Well, she could forget it. He wasn't going to risk losing his daughter to appease the woman who'd given her up in the first place.

"I don't think so, Ms. Martinson." He swung around and opened the door. "You can leave now."

"Hear me out. Please."

The pleading in her voice startled him. God, she even sounded like Mel.

He slammed the door, and she flinched. Good, let her be frightened. Because if she so much as *tried* to take his daughter away from him, he'd hunt her down and...

"I just want a chance to meet her and get to know her." Her voice was whisper soft, not at all the forceful personality he'd encountered in his two previous conversations with her.

"No." Cold and blunt, but the point was the same. *No way in hell, lady.*

Dark, finely arched brows drew together in a sleek line over bright-green eyes. "What harm can there possibly be in me at least meeting her?"

"What harm?" he roared. "Lady, are you nuts?"

"Obviously," she muttered, and turned away.

He strode across the room until he was standing directly in front of her, giving her no choice but to look up at him. A small power play, but he wasn't above using his own physical advantages at a time like this. He simply had too much to lose.

"Do you know what kind of shock it'd give her? What do I say? 'Mel, this is your birth mother. She wants to get to know you,'" he said with more than a hint of sarcasm. "No!"

Much to his amazement she didn't back down or cower. Frustration flashed in her eyes and, if he wasn't fighting for his daughter's life, he might have found her gumption just a little stimulating.

"You don't have to tell her who I am. You could tell her I'm an old friend. She doesn't even have to know I'm the one who's donated the bone marrow."

Bracing his hands on his hips, he continued to scowl at her. "And just how long do you plan on 'visiting'?" he asked against his better judgment.

She pulled in a deep breath and stepped away. "I've arranged for a month-long leave of absence."

"A month?" A few days, maybe, if that's what it took to get what Mel needed. But a month? No way could he have this woman living under the same roof with his daughter. He shook his head.

"Look Mr. Winslow. A month isn't all that long to ask for. I've lost—"

"Don't tell me what you've lost," he thundered. "You made the decision to give her up for adoption. And believe me, if Mel didn't need you for physiological reasons, you would have gone blissfully through life without knowing her."

"Haven't you ever done something you've regretted?" she asked. "She's your daughter, I just want—"

"A chance to right some cosmic wrong?" he retorted. "Forget it."

She let out a stream of breath and closed her eyes momentarily. In that instant she reminded him so much of Mel. The way her long, dark lashes fanned her cheeks, the stream of breath that ruffled bangs and spoke loud and clear of dramatic frustration.

She opened her eyes and gave him a direct stare. "Please, Mr. Winslow. There's no other way I know how to ask."

The pleading note in her voice ripped through him, and he felt himself begin to soften. He'd have to be pretty convincing where Mel was concerned. How could he just bring a strange woman into their home and pretend they were old friends?

"All I'm asking for is a month to get to know her. I don't want to upset her. I'm willing for her to never know who I really am. Won't you agree? Please, Mr. Winslow."

Sam strode to the window and stared into the horizon. He wanted to tell her to get out—to leave and forget he'd ever contacted her. But he couldn't. No matter how much he detested her manipulative tactics, for Mel he couldn't afford the luxury of telling Rebecca Martinson to go straight to hell.

"One month in exchange for bone marrow?"

Rebecca expelled a rush of breath. She was getting through to him. As cold and heartless as he made it sound, that was exactly what she wanted. "Yes," she said, not bothering to tell him that even if he'd refused she would have checked into the hospital immediately to begin the extraction process.

"One month," he repeated and turned to face her. He strode across the room until he was towering over her again. "My daughter knows she's adopted, Ms. Martinson." His soft voice belied the fury burning in his dark eyes. "God help us both if she finds out who you really are."

"FLIGHT 473, nonstop to Denver will commence boarding in five minutes."

Rebecca checked her watch for the fourth time in as many minutes. She opened her shoulder bag and retrieved the airline ticket delivered to her last night. She double-checked the flight number—473. A few hours to Denver, then a commuter to a place called Minot, North Dakota. From what Sam had told her, he lived in a small town with a population of less than five hundred. Her condo complex was more populous.

She looked at the overhead monitor and bit her lip. Their flight was due for take off in less than thirty minutes, and Sam Winslow still hadn't shown.

Turning to face the electronic doors, she watched as people flooded into the terminal at LAX. Not one of them was Sam. She sighed. How difficult could it be to spot one taller-than-average, better-looking-than-any-man-had-a-right-to-be guy with a permanent frown creasing his brow?

In this crowd, impossible.

She turned and headed toward the bank of phones intending to call his hotel. Maybe he'd overslept. If he wasn't familiar with the layout of the airport, he could even have gotten lost. She reached for the pay phone when she spotted him, walking toward her at a brisk pace. Her pulse rate picked up speed.

Pulling in a deep breath, she told herself to calm down. Her rocketing heartbeat had nothing to do with the way Sam's rich sable hair curled just right at his nape or the fact that he had the sexiest bedroom eyes she'd ever seen in her adult life. The purpose of this trip had nothing to do with Sam Winslow and everything to do with her daughter. And besides, more than likely he was a married man!

"Sorry I'm late," he said, ushering her toward the metal detector without pause. "The rental car had to be dropped off."

"No need to apologize. I only just arrived myself," she lied. She'd been waiting, and pacing, for over an hour.

Neither of them spoke, for which Rebecca was thankful. She didn't know what to say. Better to suffer through the awkward silence than put her foot in her mouth, which she'd undoubtedly do, considering she had a record-setting case of nerves. Facing the toughest judge the family court had to offer never rattled her, but the presence of one tall, drop-dead-gorgeous man she knew nothing about had the ability to make her feel like a complete klutz.

He approached the metal detector and waited for her to set her carry-on and purse on the black conveyor belt. She stepped through the electronic archway toward a security guard who passed a hand-held detector over her body. Nothing beeped or screeched so she moved on to the end of the table to await the arrival of her bags.

Sam wasn't so lucky. When he stepped through the archway, a high, piercing wail sounded. The security guard pointed him back through again. Rebecca picked up Sam's carry-all while he removed his belt and a few trinkets from the pockets of his jeans. Finally he strode toward her, took the bag from her and silently guided her toward the loading gate and aboard the plane that would take her to her daughter.

She still couldn't get over the initial surprise of finally being given the chance to meet the child she'd been forced to give up so long ago. Fate, she knew, played funny tricks on people, and sometimes righted the wrongs. She prayed again, like she had so many times in the past forty-eight hours, that this was her chance.

Once their bags were stored in the overhead compartment and they were comfortably seated, Rebecca turned to Sam. "Not much of a talker are you?"

He looked at her, and she wished she knew what he was thinking. The warmth of his eyes was a direct contrast to the creasing of his brows. She had no idea what went on in his mind. And she didn't know a thing about him. Well, maybe it was time she found out. Like how his wife was going to feel about her barging into their lives.

She gave him one of her best smiles. "I don't know anything about you."

"There isn't much to know." He adjusted his seat belt then looked past her, out the window toward the tarmac.

She wasn't about to be put off by his less-than-friendly attitude. Work. Work was always a good subject. People loved to talk about what they did for a living. "What kind of work do you do in Shelbourne, North Dakota?"

"Farming."

"You're a farmer?" She didn't mean to sound so shocked. She should have guessed him to be an outdoorsy kind of guy who worked with his hands. She remembered those hands, strong, powerful. Yet, she somehow knew they could also be tender and gentle. Tender and gentle enough to bring a woman to a fever pitch.

"Not everyone has had the advantages you've had, Ms. Martinson."

Ouch. Maybe his hands could be tender and gentle, but his attitude was sharper than a switchblade. "Don't expect me to apologize because I've had a good life. I got K through twelve just like everyone else. Just because I—"

"I'm sorry."

This guy could shift gears faster than a close-ratio Ferrari. "Excuse me?"

He sighed, then looked at her. The frown disappeared and he looked handsome again. "I said I was sorry. This situation is a little…tense."

"No kidding." She laid her hand over his strong forearm. "And you're not helping."

"You want me to make this easy for you?" Slowly, as if he didn't want her to notice, he removed his arm from her grasp.

"You don't have to make anything *easy* for anyone. We can't help where we've come from or what we've had to do to get where we are. Why don't we just accept that and go on from here, okay?"

Uh-oh. Frown's back.

"Is that what you did, Ms. Martinson? What you had to do to get where you are today?"

She glared at him. There was nothing else for her to do. She couldn't very well get up and walk out of an airplane taxiing down the runway. But she didn't want to keep suffering his sarcasm for the next three and a half hours, not to mention another ninety minutes on a rock-and-tumble commuter flight.

"Look, Winslow," she said, giving him a narrow-eyed glare as the plane lifted off. "My past is *my* past. Tough decisions were made that are pretty much none of your damn business. So why don't you just pipe down and be civil. Okay?"

His expressed immediately softened, and his dark eyes filled with contrition. "Are you always this sassy?" he asked.

"Only with people who have a rotten attitude."

"Touché," he said, the beginning of a grin tugging his lips ever so slightly.

"I bet your wife doesn't let you get away with that attitude."

"I'm not married."

"Let me guess. Your winning smile drove her away, right?" Okay, so he was right. She was sassy. But she knew all about pecking order, and she was not about to let Sam Winslow intimidate her into playing Beta to his Alpha. He might be gaining the home field advantage, but he'd learn soon enough his opponent was anything but a pushover.

This was not how Sam had planned his association with his daughter's birth mother. In fact, since he'd walked into Rebecca's office yesterday, not much had gone as planned...his physical reaction to her topping the list.

He'd seen the photograph of her and knew she was a beautiful woman, but he wasn't prepared for the sleek, cat-like grace she possessed when she moved, or the way her bright-green eyes pooled when he mentioned Mel. Nor had he been prepared for the physical response that surged through his body when she'd gently laid her hand over his arm. *That* had been a curve ball he hadn't seen coming.

An hour later Sam hadn't come to terms with the way his body had reacted to Rebecca. When the flight attendant offered them a drink, Rebecca ordered a diet cola. He wanted a double bourbon—straight, but settled for coffee instead.

He thanked the attendant and gave Rebecca his full attention. She sighed, a wistful little sound that stirred his blood.

"I don't want Mel to know you're the one to donate the bone marrow," he blurted. He'd been trying to find a tactful way to approach the subject. Oh well, he thought. At least it was out in the open.

She looked at him and lifted one of those dark brows in silent question.

"Mel's not a stupid kid," he said quietly. "A sibling or a biological parent are the most likely matches in bone marrow transplantation and she's aware of that fact. She's heard the rundown on the entire medical process and can easily figure it out for herself who you really are."

Setting her diet cola on the fold-down tray, she traced squiggles in the condensation of the plastic cup with a perfectly manicured nail. "I thought we already had this discussion."

True, he thought, but he wanted to make certain Mel was protected. "I don't lie to my kid, but in this case it's necessary. And, Ms. Martinson?" Sam waited until she looked at him. "Once the month is over, that's it. You'll never be allowed to see *my* daughter again."

A PINCUSHION had fewer holes than Rebecca did in her arm. As soon as she'd checked into the hospital, they'd sent in the legalized vampires to begin the methodical torture of withdrawing vial upon vial of blood. The nurse had threatened an IV would be started before she went to sleep. Rebecca didn't think she had a vein left for the insertion.

She continued to surf the fourteen available channels and finally landed on a local news program. While a petite blonde talked about an overturned grain truck on one of the highways, Rebecca thought about her daughter, two floors above her.

"Damn," she muttered. She never should have promised Sam she'd wait to meet Melanie until after the girl was released from the hospital. But even her promise failed to squelch the burning desire to sneak upstairs and take a look at her.

The newscaster promised a weather report after a commercial break. Melanie was probably sleeping. There certainly was nothing on television to hold one's interest, let alone that of a teenaged girl. Maybe she could just take a walk, stretch her legs and stroll past the room. If Melanie was awake, she'd keep going, but…

Unable to resist any longer, she reached for her cotton robe and pulled it around her. She jammed her feet into the slippers the nurse had parked neatly at the bedside. Firmly ignoring the possible repercussions, she left the private hospital room, strolled past the nurses' station and headed for the elevator.

After a moment the doors whooshed open, and she stepped inside, pushed the button for the fifth floor and waited. Her insides churned, and her heart pounded in a heavy rhythm. Thank goodness she was in a hospital—a crash cart would easily be at hand if she arrested.

The doors slid open, and she stepped off the elevator onto the fifth floor. Now what? she wondered. She was here, her daughter was somewhere on the floor, but where? What if Sam left instructions with the nursing staff that Melanie was to have no visitors? No Rebecca Martinson visitors?

Hesitantly she headed down the corridor toward the nurses' station. An older man, apparently a doctor, was jotting notes in a chart and giving orders to a nurse. She couldn't just walk the halls and pray she'd be guided by some magical force to her child.

Wiping her hands on the thin material of her robe, she continued toward the nurses' station.

"What about the Winslow girl?" the nurse asked.

Rebecca froze.

"She's resting comfortably," the doctor answered,

handing the chart to the nurse. "She'll be transplanted at 7:00 a.m. by Dr. Walsh."

Rebecca slowed her steps, straining to hear anything, a sliver of hope that they believed the transplant would be a success.

"I hope it works." The nurse placed the chart on the Formica counter. "She's such a—"

A high-pitched beep sounded. The nurse looked over the counter and pushed a button. "Sandy Reed again."

The doctor chuckled, then strode away while the nurse took off in the opposite direction.

The chart lay on the stark counter.

Rebecca bit her lip and hurried forward. The nurses' station was deserted. She looked over her shoulder, up and down the corridor, then scanned the chart. The name typed on the bottom of the form entitled Doctor's Orders was Mary Fitzmyer.

With another surreptitious glance around the vicinity, she made certain all was clear. A few televisions droned in the background along with the bleeps and chirps from various monitors and medical equipment. Standing on tiptoe, she peered over the counter. Medical charts lined the desk area. Valuable minutes would be wasted if she had to search each chart to see which room was Melanie's.

Another look around the area and she darted around the counter. M. Winslow. The name and room number was posted to a board with little red lights that flashed when someone required the nursing staff's attention.

Room 529.

She didn't believe it possible, but her heartbeat thudded painfully in her chest. This was it.

Wiping her damp palms on her robe a second time, she rechecked the area, then hurried from around the counter.

She checked the sign. Rooms 519 to 529. Melanie would be at the end of the corridor.

She'd come this far, she couldn't back out now. Nervously she headed toward the end of the corridor, staying close to the pale-mauve walls for support. Stopping outside the slightly opened door to room 529, she listened, barely able to hear a thing beyond the blood pounding in her ears.

Absolute quiet. No television, radio or even the sounds of a magazine or book pages being turned. With one last glance down the corridor, she quietly pushed the door open. By the soft light from the hallway spilling into the room, she spotted the bed. Curled on her side sleeping peacefully, was a tiny girl with hair as dark as Rebecca's own and a pert nose remarkably reminiscent of Rebecca's mother.

Her breath stopped, and she fought an unexpected rush of tears. This was her child, her daughter. Carefully she stepped more fully into the room and approached the bed. Melanie Winslow looked so small and fragile, Rebecca's heart broke as if it was nothing more than delicate crystal smashed cruelly against the pavement. She deeply resented that she'd had to give this beautiful child away, but her father hadn't given her a choice.

Dwelling on the past solved nothing. She had to look to the future, grateful to have the one month Sam had granted her.

The girl stirred. Rebecca held her breath as realization flooded her. God, what had she done? If Melanie awakened and found her here, how would she explain her presence later? She'd promised Sam she wouldn't do this—and look at her, sneaking around the hospital in the middle of the night.

Melanie snuggled further beneath the blankets, and Rebecca expelled the breath she'd been holding. As carefully and as quietly as possible she backed out of the room and pulled the door near closed.

By the time she reached her room, her limbs trembled uncontrollably. Personal risks were something she rarely employed. Gambling was not on her list of habits, but she'd certainly done more than her fair share in the past forty-eight hours. She knew getting to know Melanie was risky—she could lose, and the cost was astronomical. She'd suffered heartache once. Did she really think she could bear to suffer it again?

Chapter Three

The textbooks lied. There was no other explanation for the horrible throbbing pain in her hips. Rebecca winced when Sam swerved to avoid another pothole in the road. She didn't think the bruises would ever fade, considering the coat hanger they'd used to extract bone marrow the previous day.

The radio played softly, a country-western station no less, and she wondered if they played other types of music out here in the middle of nowhere. She doubted Sam even owned anything remotely close to classical music, unless one considered Hank Williams classical, she thought crankily.

Occasional farmhouses and huge red or white barns dotted the sprawling countryside as they headed north toward the Canadian border. A few corrals with a horse or two grazing idly, and even small paddocks with cattle, now and then broke up the vast landscape, but mainly her view consisted of field upon field of wheat and other types of soon-to-be grains she didn't recognize.

As they passed a field of sunflowers, Rebecca marveled at the huge, bright-yellow flowers, all facing in the same easterly direction, like smart little soldiers waiting in ranks for the order to march forward into battle. She thought of asking Winslow how they did that, but he'd been silent and sullen since they'd left the hospital so she kept her questions to herself.

"How much farther is it to Shelbourne?" she asked twenty minutes later, more out of boredom than anything else. She shifted in her seat and stifled a groan when her sweats rubbed uncomfortably against her bruised hipbone.

"Another forty minutes or so." Sam kept his eyes trained on the flat roadway. Other than the rich tenor on the radio singing about putting the past behind him, the cab was silent again.

"Did you make reservations for me?" she asked, feeling more uncomfortable by the minute. Not only was Sam's less-than-friendly attitude beginning to wear on her nerves, she wanted nothing more than to lie down.

"Reservations?"

She sighed. "Yeah. You know, like in a hotel? A place where I can rest my head at night? Or did you plan on stuffing me in a hay-filled stall with all the other barnyard animals?"

He tossed an exasperated glance her way. "The closest *motel* is fifty miles away from the farm. You'll be staying at the house with us."

She sat up and winced. "What?"

"Sorry, Ms. Martinson, but Shelbourne isn't exactly a mecca filled with fine restaurants and five-star hotels."

Rebecca turned to the window, worrying her lower lip. She'd imagined spending her time in a nice little hotel room, going with Sam to visit Melanie and waiting for word that the transplant was indeed the success the preliminary reports were showing. Once the doctors released Melanie to home care, she'd envisioned spending a few days a week at the house playing the role of visitor—not taking up residence with Witty Winslow.

Thirty minutes later they turned from the highway onto a secondary road. They passed the tall cylinders of a grain elevator and finally a silver tower with the word Shelbourne painted in black, block-style letters.

She shielded her eyes from the bright North Dakota sunshine and struggled to sit straighter to get a look at the town where her daughter lived. Sam slowed the truck to the twenty-five-mile-per-hour speed limit posted for the city limits.

City? she wondered silently. *City* wasn't exactly the word she would use to describe the three-block section of Shelbourne. There was a hardware store, a post office, a grocery with big red letters that said just that and a drugstore, all in one block. The next block boasted a beauty shop she was certain Ron, her stylist, would flay her alive if she dared to visit. On the other side of the street stood a floral shop, an auto parts store and a barbershop, complete with an old-fashioned red-and-white pole. There were a couple of taverns, a place called the Shelbourne Diner and at the end of the street a mechanic's shop that doubled as a gas station. Before she could blink, they'd crossed over a set of railroad tracks and then more wide-open nothingness. Just more fields of summer crops.

"That's it?" she asked, and turned to look behind her. There hadn't been a police station, city hall, not even a library or a church. "Where's the police station?"

"We don't have one," he answered, and she could hear the smile in his voice.

"You guys dish out justice Western style, or what?"

He chuckled and the sound swept over her, stirring her senses. "No. We have a county sheriff in a nearby town. There's a courthouse, too, a couple of lawyers, a medical clinic. Pretty much everything we need is here in Shelbourne or Johnstone. For anything else I travel to Minot once a month."

"I see." Really she didn't. Where were the convenience stores? Or a movie theater, or video store? God, where did Melanie go if she got a craving for a hot-fudge sundae? Canada?

She turned her gaze back to Sam. "You said it was a small town, but cripes, I didn't realize you meant it."

"Feeling a little out of your element, Ms. Martinson?'' There was no animosity in his voice, just mild amusement which made her smile.

''Actually...yes,'' she admitted, curious to know what Melanie did for recreation in a town the size of Shelbourne.

Sam didn't reply, but turned the truck onto a gravel road. Instinctively she clutched the dashboard in an effort to keep the jarring to a minimum. As if he sensed her discomfort, he thankfully slowed the truck and she relaxed. She hoped he had a comfortable bed for her. Her hips were killing her, and she was exhausted. The doctor had warned her to take it easy for a week. Considering what she'd just seen of the town, she didn't think that was going to be a problem, because Sam had been right. Shelbourne was not exactly a mecca.

WHEN SAM HAD SAID he was a simple farmer, Rebecca envisioned a little red barn in need of repair on the edge of a wheat field. She imagined cows and pigs, chickens pecking the ground, maybe even a small corral for a horse or two along with a big lazy bloodhound snoozing in the shade.

The dusty driveway she'd pictured was in reality a smooth concrete drive bordered by majestic evergreens. Replacing the little red barn of her imagination stood a monstrosity of red, neatly trimmed in white, along with three other long, low, rounded buildings of equal size. There were other outbuildings, as well, each painted white with a red *W* above the doors. She counted close to two dozen huge, galvanized-steel cylinders along a treeline and varying types of heavy machinery she couldn't begin to name.

Sam drove past the barn and outbuildings and waved to a group of at least a dozen men resting on benches beneath the shade of a large maple tree. But the sight that stole her breath was the farmhouse itself, the house she would share with Sam and Melanie for the next four weeks.

She'd prepared herself for the worst, imagining a clapboard shack with peeling paint, a sagging roof and dusty windows. The structure that loomed in front of her could only be referred to as stately. The home was subdued elegance and country comfort, a combination she never would have been able to imagine. A covered porch swept across the front, complete with an old-fashioned wooden railing that made her think of warm summer evenings and sunsets. A bed of spring flowers strained toward the warmth of the sun, creating a picture-postcard effect she found too enchanting for words.

A tall, reed-thin man sauntered from around the side of the house, a cowboy hat shielding his eyes from the sun. His weathered face broke into a grin as he approached them. "Boy am I glad you're here. We've got a small problem, Sam."

Sam slipped a blue ball cap onto his head and slid from the truck. "What's up, Jake?"

"It's that old combine again," he said. "R.D.'s

won't have the parts in until next week, and I can't spare a man to run into the city right now.''

"Damn." Sam braced his hands on his denim-clad hips. "That wheat's ready to come down. We need every piece of equipment in those fields."

Jake tilted his hat back, exposing thick salt-and-pepper hair. "I did another grain test this morning, boss. I've started the boys out there today in the far northern square."

"Have you called around to see if anyone can get the parts to us?"

Jake nodded. "Farm Supply in the city, but they can't deliver until Friday. I'd head off but we've already got four truckloads of grain ready to take to the elevator and we're short a driver."

Carefully Rebecca opened the door to the cab and stepped onto the driveway. Sam and his foreman could have been speaking a foreign language. She didn't have a clue what they were talking about, but she could tell from the dark expression on Sam's face he wasn't too happy.

She closed the door, and both men turned to look in her direction.

Jake touched the brim of his cowboy hat. "Ma'am."

"Rebecca Martinson, this is Jake Henshaw. He's my foreman."

She walked around the front of the pickup and extended her hand to Jake. "A pleasure, Mr. Henshaw."

Jake chuckled and shook her hand. "Just Jake, ma'am. You a friend of Sam's?"

"We're old friends from college." The lie easily slid from her lips, from where, she couldn't be sure. She supposed it was the safest and most logical explanation for her presence at Winslow Farms.

She caught Sam's dark gaze, but his eyes revealed nothing.

"I've got to head back into the city," Sam told her. "I hope you don't mind."

"Not at all." She'd been worried about what they would find to talk about. His abrupt departure would at least give her a chance to find her bearings. "I'll just get settled, if you'll show me where I'll be staying."

Sam said a few more words to Jake and sent the older man to call in the order so it would be ready when he arrived.

"This way." He inclined his head toward the side of the house and pulled her overnight bag from the bed of the truck.

Rebecca followed him up a short set of steps into a utility room the size of a small office. An antique bench butted against the wall next to a rack filled with boots and shoes. Inside of an open closet space, coats and sweaters hung neatly on a bar below a shelf with a variety of hats, gloves and scarves.

When she stepped into the kitchen, she stared in amazement. Most people thought of the kitchen as the heart of a home. To her, it had always been the room where she kept the cereal and microwave dinners. Just about every appliance, small and large, most of which she couldn't begin to name, adorned the spacious, cream ceramic-tiled counters. A large oval oak table held center stage atop an authentic brick floor. Rich oak cabinets with matching ceramic handles or knobs, along with braided oval rugs, cream lace curtains and baskets filled with dried or silk flowers added a comfortable down-home feel to an otherwise technologically sterile environment.

"Mel's idea," he said, nodding to the feminine touches.

He dropped her bag on a thick-legged chair near the table. "Make yourself at home," he said, removing his cap and running his fingers through his hair. "I had your bags brought upstairs yesterday. Your room is the third door on the left. You'll find leftovers in the fridge if you get hungry." He glanced at his watch then slapped his cap back on his head. "I should be back in time for supper."

Back in time for supper? Oh, sweet heaven. He didn't expect her to cook, did he? Because she had serious doubts that her one speciality, Rebecca *raman,* would be well received in the land of meat and potatoes. Before she could ask Sam, he spun on his heel and disappeared through the utility room.

Sam drove away before she pulled out a chair and sat. Now what? She was miles from home, exhausted, and didn't have the first clue what to do with herself.

Resting her elbow on the heavy table, she plopped her chin in her hand.

What was she doing here?

Maybe she should leave. Victor had been right, she had no business coming to North Dakota. She should ask Sam's foreman to take her back to the airport and she could jump on the first plane back to California. Open adoptions were becoming more and more common, but she always advised her adoption clients not to maintain contact with the birth mother because ultimately, the child suffered. She knew the arguments by rote, but her heart cried out for this one chance to get to know the daughter she'd lost. The choice of keeping her child had been taken away from her when she'd been a mere child herself. How could she turn away from the opportunity she now held in her hands?

No. She couldn't think about what might go wrong. Melanie was not going to find out who she really was, and after her month was up, she'd leave.

And do what? she asked herself.

Learn to live her life without her child—all over again.

THREE HOURS LATER Sam still hadn't returned. Rebecca had showered, changed and explored the large and elegant farmhouse and was bored stiff. Needing something to occupy her time, she found her way to the kitchen. Sam said he'd be home for supper. What time was supper in North Dakota? She'd seen for herself that the sun didn't set until after nearly eleven o'clock each night. And she'd already learned that lunch was called dinner, which she didn't think she'd ever get used to hearing. Things were certainly different in the Midwest.

Well, maybe she wasn't much of a cook, but she did have quite a knack for microwave dinners. Sam said there were leftovers. Maybe she could warm some of those and they'd eat *supper* together.

With some effort she located the makings of what she deemed a decent meal. Now all she had to do was figure out how to operate the electric stove, since Sam didn't have a microwave, which she thought odd considering the multitude of gadgets in his kitchen.

Geeze, what did Melanie do for popcorn? she wondered.

Twenty minutes later, and after several false starts, she'd sliced a leftover roast, found a container with what she thought could pass for gravy and set them to simmer. She wrinkled her nose. Warming, the meat had a strange odor.

She peered into the skillet. It looked like roast beef. Checking the container, she found a masking tape label on the lid with a *V* printed on the top. "Veal?" she murmured, and looked back in the pan. Didn't look, or smell, like any veal she'd ever seen. With a shrug she padded across the brick floor to the freezer, hoping to find some vegetables. Stacked inside in neat orderly rows were meats, clearly labeled and wrapped in white paper. She found hamburger, T-bones, roasts, pork chops and...

"Venison! Oh my, God. I'm cooking *Bambi!*"

With a disgusted cry, she slammed the freezer door then hurried across the kitchen as quickly as possible, considering her sore hip. She snapped off the burner and glared at the contents in the skillet. No way was she eating *Bambi*.

Now what? she thought. She returned to the fridge and found some lettuce and tomatoes. She added a can of tuna she found in the pantry and successfully turned it into a salad. Now her only problem was she couldn't find a drop of dressing. She vaguely recalled a cooking show she'd seen once when she was stuck in bed with the flu for a week. Maybe she could make her own salad dressing. After locating cooking oil and a bottle of vinegar, she dumped the contents of both bottles into a bowl, stirred them, then set the bowl in the fridge to chill.

Happy with her endeavors, she wandered to the family room and flipped on the television. She found an old movie and settled on the sofa to wait for Sam.

MELANIE SAT against a mound of pillows, a teen magazine propped in her lap when Sam walked through the door. For the first time in weeks a hint of sparkle shone in her eyes.

Overcome by a rush of emotion, he stopped and stared at his daughter. He'd been so afraid he would lose her. First the unknown, and then the dreaded diagnosis that forced him to locate her birth mother. Thanks to Rebecca, Mel now had a chance. For that, he would always be grateful to her.

"Dad!" Mel tossed the magazine aside. "I'm *so* bored."

Sam chuckled at her melodramatics and produced the stuffed bear he'd been holding behind his back, before sitting on the edge of the bed. "That's a good sign."

Mel gave him one of her breathtaking grins. Shock rippled through him. That smile he'd always loved on his daughter reminded him too much of Rebecca. Mother and daughter shared the same smile, the same hair and eye color, but that's where the physical similarities ended. He'd always had a mild curiosity about Mel's parentage. Since meeting Rebecca, that curiosity had mounted, almost to the point of obsession.

Mel wrapped her slender arms around his neck and gave him a fierce hug. "Thanks for the bear, Dad."

"Anytime."

Mel settled against the pillows and hugged the pink teddy to her chest. "What are you doing here? I called the house. Where were you?"

"You called the house?" Rebecca was at the house.

"Yeah, I left a message on the machine. I figured you were busy with harvest."

Sam breathed a sigh of relief. He'd have to explain Rebecca's presence sooner or later, but he preferred later. "I had to come in to the city to pick up a part for one of the combines. The boys have already started taking down the wheat."

A flicker of sadness flashed in her green eyes. "I guess that means you won't be able to come see me tomorrow, huh?"

He'd never disappointed his daughter, and he wasn't about to start now. Harvest or no harvest. "I'll be here, Mel. I promise."

"That's okay, Dad," she said, giving him a half smile. "I know you'll be busy. You don't have to."

True, harvest time was difficult, with long hours from sunup until sundown. Most times they never even came in from the fields for meals. In the past, his widowed mother had helped out at harvest, bringing meals to the hands twice a day, and keeping up with the household chores, but last fall she'd relocated to Arizona to live with her sister in the much warmer climate. He needed to hire a housekeeper and cook, test the durum and canola fields, and deal with a mountain of paperwork piling up on his desk, but nothing could keep him from getting away to spend time with Mel until she came home, even if he could only manage to get away for a few hours at a time.

"I'll be here," he told her again.

Mel pushed a length of raven's-wing hair over her shoulder. "Did you hear the good news, Dad? Dr. Walsh said I might be able to come home this weekend."

He'd spoken to the doctor before coming in to see

Mel. Granted, she might be released by the weekend, but that meant she'd need to come to the city three times a week to be monitored. With harvesting, he wasn't sure how he was going to be able to do everything, both at home and with Mel. But he'd find a way. He and Mel had always made it, and they weren't about to stop now.

"Dad?" Melanie peeked at him through long dark lashes, her hands folded in her lap.

He was in trouble. His daughter was anything but the demure picture she was attempting to paint. He gave her a stern look. "What?"

She leaned forward, placing her small hands on his arm. "Since I missed my driver's ed classes this summer, can I take private lessons at one of those schools?"

He let out a pent up breath. The last thing he wanted right now was his daughter driving. "Let's wait until you get home to discuss this."

"Please, Dad," she pleaded. "Leah's taking her test next week. She'll have her license before me."

"It's not the end of the world, Mel."

She sat back and crossed her arms over her chest. "Yes it is. I'll be the only ninth-grader *without* a driver's license."

"We'll see."

"That's not an answer," she said, pouting.

"It's the only answer you're going to get right now." He slid his finger down the slope of her nose, softening the rebuke.

Melanie sighed, her expression turning serious. "You know, I've been thinking a lot lately."

"About what this time?" he asked, checking his watch. Jake was waiting for the parts to repair the combine.

"I'd like to see my mother."

Sam stared at Mel, not knowing what to say. As soon as she'd been old enough to understand, he'd told her she was adopted. The question of her birth mother had never come up—until now.

"Your mother?" he asked when he found his voice.

"I hope you're not upset, Dad. But I've been thinking about her a lot lately. I don't remember much about her."

Sam breathed a sigh of relief. She wasn't referring to Rebecca, but Christina, her *adoptive* mother. The mother who walked out on her when she was six years old.

"Baby, I don't even know where she is. I haven't seen her since she—" *turned her back on us.* Regardless of his feelings, or lack of them, for Christina, she was the only mother Mel knew. By the time Mel was ten, she'd given up looking for birthday cards and Christmas cards from her mother. Not a single word. Why Mel would even want to see her baffled him, but Christina was a fickle woman and might one day rediscover her maternal instincts. If that happened, he didn't want to color Mel's vision in that regard. "Since she left," he continued. "You know that."

"What about my grandparents? Wouldn't they know where she is?"

"What is this all about?"

She lowered her gaze and began plucking at the blanket. "I thought she might come see me when I was sick. I guess I want to ask her why she doesn't love me."

He hooked his finger under her chin until she was looking at him. "I love you. And in her own way, I'm sure your mother does, too. She just wasn't an openly affectionate person, Mel."

Tears pooled in her eyes, breaking Sam's heart. He could handle almost any situation, but Mel's tears had the ability to reduce his heart to shreds.

"Did I do something to make her leave? Was it because she wasn't my *real* mother?" Her whispered questions ate at his conscience. He preached honesty above all else to his daughter, but he couldn't tell her—he wouldn't hurt her like that.

"Your mother and I divorced because we wanted different things in life. It had nothing to do with you." That was at least partially true. They *had* wanted different things. While Sam was content managing the land and providing for his family, Christina had dreams of grandeur. She'd hated their life on the farm—often calling him, and the people he'd known all his life, nothing more than dirt farmers.

He'd hoped having a child would make her happy.

But after five years of failed attempts and three miscarriages, they'd given up hope and agreed to adopt. Too late, Christina admitted she'd wanted her own child—not some other woman's leavings, as she'd said during their last heated argument. If the truth were told, Christina resented the hell out of Mel. His daughter was a constant reminder of the one thing Christina could not have—her own children.

A lone, hot tear slid down Mel's cheek, and he wiped it with the pad of his thumb. It reminded him of other tears, of strangled cries in the middle of the night, of holding his daughter until her tears had been spent and she finally rested. It reminded him of the day Christina walked out and never looked back.

He gathered her in his arms and wished he could spend the rest of the afternoon with her, but Jake was waiting for him. God, he hated to leave her, wishing he could stay in the city until she was ready to come home, but he had a business to operate and a mountain of medical bills that wouldn't get paid if they didn't get the crop in and to market. Too bad he had the type of business that couldn't be run from seventy miles away.

"I want you to think about getting well and coming home." He placed a kiss against her head and heard her sniffle. "Everyone misses you."

She pulled away. "I love you, Dad."

"I love you, too," he said, releasing her. "I've got to get back. But I'll call you later. Okay?"

Mel wiped the tears from her face with the back of

her hand. "Okay," she said, and gave him a shaky grin.

He stood and looked down at Mel. A small glimmer of hope rose to soothe his tired nerves. His daughter *would* be coming home.

The only problem was, a new set of troubles awaited him. Mel's birth mother. What did she really want? Were her manipulative tactics simply a ruse to worm her way into Mel's life? Or were her reasons as she'd stated, only wanting to meet Mel, assure herself she'd made the right decision all those years ago?

Unless he confronted her, he'd never know. And he needed to know before Mel came home.

The time had come to demand a few answers from Mel's birth mother.

Chapter Four

Sam pulled into the drive, jammed the truck into park and bolted from the cab. Smoke billowed from the open kitchen window at the back of the house. With his heart pounding, he threw open the door and was hit by the odor of acrid smoke and burning meat.

"Rebecca!"

Dear God, what had happened? Waving the smoke from his face, he found the problem. An unwatched skillet burned to a crisp.

He flipped off the stove and grabbed a pot holder to carry the charred remains of the skillet to the sink.

"Rebecca!"

She hadn't been feeling all that great when he left for the city. Had something happened to her?

"Oh, my God!"

Sam turned at the sound of her voice. She looked sleepy, rumpled and sexy, as if she'd just crawled from bed. The thought sent a surge of heat to his groin.

"What were you doing?" he snapped. "Trying to burn down the house?"

She pushed her long, loose hair from her eyes. "I fell asleep. Oh, God. I'm so sorry. I'll buy you a new pan."

"I don't care about the skillet. You could've..." Could have what? Been hurt? He shouldn't have been worried about her, but dammit, she'd scared him half to death.

She approached and peered around him, a frown marring her forehead. "I thought I turned it off," she said, her voice filled with wonder.

He caught her scent, a mixture of musky cologne and feminine allure that was hers alone. "How long ago was this?" He had to keep his mind on the conversation, not the sweet sexy fragrance of the woman who had the power to destroy his life.

She looked at her watch and gave him a sheepish grin. "Almost an hour and a half."

He dropped the pan in the sink and glared at her.

"I thought I turned it off. I'm really sorry."

Sam sighed. He had enough on his mind without having to worry about Rebecca Martinson setting his house on fire, let alone the way she was making him feel right now with her voice all husky from sleep.

"Are you hungry? I made a tuna salad for dinner," she said, stepping away from him.

"What *was* this?" he asked, looking into the ruined fry pan. He supposed anyone could make a mistake, particularly if they were unaccustomed to an electric range.

"Bambi."

"What?"

She pulled two bowls from the refrigerator and sighed. "Venison," she said, wrinkling her nose.

He shrugged. What was wrong with deer meat? Christina had been the same way, he recalled, refusing to even cook the game he'd brought home during hunting season. She just hadn't looked as adorable as Rebecca when she wrinkled her nose.

Rebecca set the bowls on the table. "Where do you keep your salad plates?"

Sam pushed aside the lace curtains Mel had insisted he buy to allow more fresh air into the still-smoky kitchen. After he retrieved plates and forks, along with a loaf of fresh wheat bread that his neighbor Carrie Harrison had baked for him, they sat at the kitchen table. Rebecca dished up the salad and handed him the dressing.

He ladled the dressing over the lettuce, tomatoes and tuna, tore off a piece of bread and dipped it in the dressing. The bitter tang of vinegar attacked his taste buds and he winced.

Rebecca Martinson may be beautiful, she may even have saved his daughter's life, but she was no cook.

"Come on," he croaked, pushing away from the table.

Her delicate brows furrowed. "Something wrong?"

He took his time clearing his throat. "Uh…" He didn't want to hurt her feelings, but what could he say? "I feel like a steak. There's a steak house in Johnstone," he improvised, carrying his plate to the sink.

"Besides, it's still too smoky in here." He exaggerated by waving his hand in front of his face. "Maybe by the time we get back, it'll have cleared up a bit."

REBECCA SMILED HER THANKS at the waitress who laid a thick loaf of fresh, crusty bread on the table along with a crock of butter and two bowls filled with garden salad. The atmosphere in the steak house combined down-home comfort with rustic charm. This was provided by a display of antique tins and metal serving platters of a bygone era, rough-hewn wooden shelves and beams and an abundance of trailing plants. After a small glass of white zinfandel, she'd finally started to relax a little in Sam's company.

He picked up his knife and cut into the larger pieces of lettuce, tomato and cucumber. "Do you mind if I ask why you told Jake we were old friends from college?"

"It just slipped out," she told him, setting her glass on the red-and-white-checked tablecloth. "Please tell me you did go to college and that I haven't blown it already."

His brief nod filled her with relief. "University of

Michigan,'' he said, ''on a partial football scholarship. What about you?''

''Notre Dame.''

He lifted a brow at that one.

''I went to Ann Arbor a few times when I was a kid. I could probably fake my way through, if someone questioned it. What was your major?'' she asked, hoping to gain a little insight into the man she'd be living with for the next four weeks.

Sam reached for a roll and slathered it with freshly churned butter. ''Preveterinary medicine,'' he finally answered with an unexpected sense of longing for what would never be.

''You're a vet?'' she asked, a note of surprise in her voice.

''No. I'm the oldest of four kids,'' he said, shifting his gaze from her sparkling green eyes to the brick hearth. ''I never finished my last year of college. My dad had a heart attack and since there was no one else to take over the farm, it became my responsibility.''

He didn't bother to explain how his younger brothers had gone on to college and obtained their postgraduate degrees or that his sister was a psych major at Florida State. Nor did he explain what his decision had done to his marriage or his own dreams. Like Rebecca had said on the plane, their pasts were their own.

''I'm sorry,'' she said quietly.

''There's no reason for you to apologize,'' he said. He waited while the waitress delivered their meal and collected their half-eaten salads before continuing. "I've been thinking that maybe we should create a past. In case anyone asks." He despised lying, but in this instance there was no other choice. Not if he wanted to save Mel, not to mention himself, truckloads of heartache down the line.

She picked up her knife and cut into the country-fried steak. "Okay," she said. "How did we meet?"

He took a sip of beer, then set the bottle back on the table. "How about we had classes together?" he suggested, settling back into the chair. "You were flunking out of biology so we became study partners."

Her smile was quick and her eyes flashed with humor. Damn, if his gut didn't tighten when her entire face lit up when she smiled at him like that…like they really were old friends.

"I have *never* flunked anything in my entire life, Winslow. Try again."

"We were just friends," he said, enjoying her smile and the humor in her voice a whole lot more than he should. As if he didn't have everything to lose, his gaze roved and he lazily appraised her. With her hair pulled back in a simple ponytail and not a lick of makeup to hide her natural beauty, she was ten times more enticing than when he'd first walked into her office. The understanding and compassion that had filled her gaze when he'd told her about having to drop out of school warred with the image he'd created of the real Rebecca Martinson—a cold-blooded, heartless woman capable of giving her baby away to strangers. He didn't like to think he could be wrong. It was safer for all of them if he believed her callous and unfeeling.

"You said Melanie was a smart kid," she said, dragging her steak through the gravy on her plate. "You can do better than 'just friends.'"

"Okay, how about we dated for a while but we were better as friends."

She chuckled, a low husky sound that did strange things to his libido. "No chemistry, huh, Winslow?"

"No," he stated firmly, but wondered briefly if he was merely attempting to convince himself. No one would believe there was no chemistry between them, not in a million years. Not the way his body reacted to a simple smile or a husky laugh from this woman.

"Well, that shouldn't be all that tough," she said in that sassy tone of hers he was beginning to suspect was more of a mask for the real Rebecca. She wanted the world to think she was tough. Sam was gaining an altogether different impression, and he wasn't sure how that made him feel.

"You would have known Christina, my ex-wife. We were married in college."

"What was she like?"

He wanted to say his ex-wife was a lot like her, but he wasn't so sure any longer. They came from the same type of background, but over the past two days he was beginning to think the two women had little in common. Rebecca was ambitious, a career-minded woman. Christina's ambitions had extended little beyond herself.

"Rich, spoiled," he admitted without hesitation. "A typical daddy's girl who pouted when she didn't get her way."

"Well, let's make this easy. We can say I didn't like her much. Once you married and left school, we lost contact."

"Okay. What about you? Is there anything in your life I should know about?" There was a lot about Rebecca Martinson he *wanted* to know about. Like why she gave up her baby. And why she'd basically blackmailed him into letting her spend time with Mel.

She shrugged. "I was married for a while, but it didn't work out. He's remarried, but we're still friends." There was no sadness in her voice. She simply stated facts that he'd memorized from the private investigator's report.

She reached for her wineglass and took a sip. "I'm a junior partner at the firm and head of the Family Law Department," she said setting her glass aside. "I've applied for a judgeship, which means I'm next on the list when there's an opening in family court."

"What about your family?" He knew the basics— her background read like a *Who's Who in Washington.* But he wanted particulars—who *was* Rebecca Martinson?

"We're not close." Her tone was cold and biting, and as glacial as the look in her eyes. There was *definitely* more to Rebecca than he'd first imagined. And he was determined to find out everything about her, telling himself his reasons had nothing whatsoever to do with his physical reaction to the beautiful woman seated across from him, and everything to do with protecting his daughter.

"I should know a little about them," he said, despite the No Trespassing sign she'd just posted. "If we're going to convince Mel."

She looked away, her gaze locked on something outside the big picture window of the steak house. Obviously, she didn't wish to discuss her family, but if they were going to pull off the ruse of college pals, shouldn't he know more than what the investigator's report locked in his desk had told him?

"Rebecca?" When he'd gone from Ms. Martinson to Rebecca, he couldn't say, but her name was beginning to have a familiar ring to his ears.

Rebecca's heart jolted and her pulse pounded at the soft way he called her name. Something intense flared to life inside her, and she fought to push it away. This man disturbed her, in more ways than one.

With a gusty sigh, she turned to face him again. "My father's a state supreme court justice. My mother's a cardiovascular surgeon. My brother is a congressman with his eye on the Senate," she recited by rote. "The Martinsons come from a long line of legal eagles who are politically active. My mother's side of the family consists of familiar names in the medical journals. Overachievers run rampant in my family."

"And you're following right in their footsteps."

In spite of herself she tensed. "Actually, no," she said with more disdain than she'd intended. "I've been a disappointment to my father for a long time."

Keeping with the Martinson tradition, she'd majored in political science, but she'd followed her heart by going into practice as a family law attorney. Regardless of her status as partner and head of the department, or her possible appointment to family court judge, her father still managed to tell her that her talents lay elsewhere, like the political arena. But she despised politicians and everything they stood for. Ethics meant nothing to the rich and powerful that her father called his friends.

"My mother was brokenhearted that I chose law over medicine, but she'd never admit it to my father. No one admits anything to my father that he doesn't want to hear."

There was no love lost between her and her father, and that saddened her. Thank heavens her own daughter's relationship with her adoptive father was strong. And that thought gave her comfort.

REBECCA COULDN'T REMEMBER the last time she'd heard a serenade of crickets. For that matter, she couldn't remember a time when she'd had nothing to do but enjoy a cool evening breeze and gaze at the stars blanketing the night sky. There were no court appearances to wade through in the morning, no custody battles to prepare for and no phone calls to return. If she wasn't so exhausted, she'd probably be feeling a little antsy with nothing to do.

She checked her watch. Ten-thirty and the sun had only started to set. For the first time since she'd arrived in North Dakota, she'd begun to relax. She'd even enjoyed Sam's company at dinner. A little too much, she thought.

She inhaled a deep breath of clean air and pushed off the porch railing. Strolling across the veranda to the steps, she sat and listened to the sound of Sam's deep, rich voice carrying through the open window as he talked on the phone to Melanie. She tried not to think about the relationship Sam shared with his daughter. And she tried not to compare it to her relationship, or lack of one, with her own father.

Her father had been a strict and impatient disciplinarian who had provided well for his children. Rebecca and her older brother, Rafe, had had the best clothes, the best cars and the best education money could buy. But deep in her heart she'd wanted the one thing her father wasn't capable of giving—the kind of closeness Sam shared with Melanie. The fact was, Albert Martinson was a difficult man to know, and even harder to love. And the more she'd tried to please him, the more she'd managed to disappoint him. A fact he continually reminded her of.

The screen door snapped closed, pulling Rebecca from the direction her thoughts had taken. Turning, she watched Sam move toward her and lean against the column above the steps. His towering frame blocked the soft glow of the porch light and cast them in shadows. A ball cap shielded his eyes, but she could feel his gaze on her. A shiver that had nothing to do with the cool breeze ran through her. With her feet propped on the lower step, she protectively pulled her knees close to her chest and wrapped her arms around them.

Anxious to break the uncomfortable silence, she asked, "How is she doing?"

Sam pushed away from the column and moved down the steps. He casually propped a booted foot on the lower step and leaned against the railing. She looked up at him in time to see the flare of a match touch the tip of a cigarette. She didn't know he smoked. Granted, they hadn't spent much time together in the past couple of days, but she was still surprised.

"Her spirits are up." He tossed the dead match into the flower bed, then dragged deep on the cigarette. "I talked to her doctor. She'll be home in a few days, but she'll need to be monitored closely with regular trips to town for a while."

"She's going to be okay? The transplant is a success?"

He kept his gaze in the distance. "They try not to be too optimistic, but they're hopeful. The preliminary tests show strong progress. I'll know more tomorrow, and if all goes well, Friday, I'll bring her home."

Despite his encouraging response, she detected his

concern. This man loved his child, a child who wasn't even his biologically, but no one could say that Sam Winslow was not Melanie's father where it mattered most—the heart. Before she could stop herself, she reached across the small expanse separating them and rested her hand on his arm. "I'm glad, Sam. I'm glad I was able to help."

He pulled away from her and turned toward the open fields. She should say something, find a way to express her gratitude for the time she'd been granted, but the right words escaped her.

"I should be grateful to you, Rebecca, and don't get me wrong, I am extremely grateful." He sighed, then turned to face her. "But there's a part of me that resents the hell out of you right now."

"I think I understand," she returned quietly. Melanie was *his* daughter in every way that mattered, but he wasn't capable of giving the child he loved what she'd so desperately needed. She was certain it rankled him that a total stranger was able to give something so vitally important to Melanie. A parent was supposed to protect and provide for their child. If the situation was reversed, she imagined she'd resent him, too.

"Do you?" he asked, then lifted the cigarette to his lips again. "How can you possibly know what I'm going through right now?"

She tried to maintain her patience despite his slightly roughened tone. "I think I do," she said carefully. She *wanted* to understand him, but she also thought he should at least attempt to reciprocate on the appreciation issue. He really had no right to be angry with her. Granted, she'd forced his hand and practically blackmailed him into allowing her the one month with her daughter, but, she didn't *have* to do anything. She could have thrown him out of her office and told him never to darken her doorstep again. But she was here because it was right, regardless of the turmoil he'd brought into her life.

"You think you do," he scoffed. He tossed the half-burned cigarette onto the walkway and ground it beneath his boot. "The logical part of me knows there isn't a judge around who would let you take my daughter away from me after raising her for fourteen years. But I can't help wondering what you really want."

Rebecca looked at him, wishing he'd remove the ball cap so she could see his eyes. "I just want a chance to meet her." She had no intention of taking Melanie away from him. She might be Melanie's birth mother, but she would never harm an innocent child. Melanie belonged with Sam. *He* was her father.

He rubbed at the back of his neck. "I hope you understand that I'm having a hard time accepting that."

"I do," she answered, lifting her head. "And there isn't any other explanation, Sam." At least none that was easy or that she could use to make him understand what she was feeling. She didn't completely understand her reasons herself. Except maybe a masochistic tendency for emotional self-destruction, she thought sardonically.

"What do you want?" he demanded suddenly, his voice hard and unyielding.

"I told you," she said slowly, shocked by his sudden burst of anger. "I—"

"I'm sorry," he said even more abruptly, then took a deep breath. "Why all of a sudden, Rebecca? I'm trying to understand. You walked away and never tried to find her. Why now was it so important to see her? You must want something."

She looked away, but the movement did nothing to lessen the hurt crowding her chest. Damn him for making her dredge up the past. The memories, the pain, the nightmare that had been her life fifteen years before. She'd thought she'd come to terms with her circumstances years ago, but Sam's gentle interrogation resurrected old hurts like Lazarus rising from the tomb.

"I wasn't given a choice when Melanie was born," she said quietly. She had no ulterior motives to confess, but that didn't mean she'd never thought about the child, wondered if she'd been safe and in a good, loving home. Was it so wrong for her to want to see these things for herself?

Sam removed the ball cap and pushed his hand through his hair. Frustration nudged him. She wasn't making sense. Of course she'd had a choice. Didn't she? "What do you mean you didn't have a choice?"

Abruptly, she stood. From her perch on the steps

she was eye level with him, and he had no trouble discerning the heated glare in her clear green eyes along with a hefty dose of something else that reminded him of pain.

"My family thought adoption would be the best thing for the child," she said in a sharp tone.

"The best thing for the child—or for you?"

"What does it matter now? Over fourteen years ago, a decision was made. *I've* learned to live with it."

"Your family made the decision for you?" he asked incredulously.

"That's right, Winslow. Believe it or not, even in a family full of brilliant legal minds who argued case law at the dinner table, things like a woman's legal right to choose was not an option. Not for me, anyway."

He shook his head. "What happened? The high-and-mighty Martinson family couldn't bear up under the pressure of a bastard in their family tree, huh?"

She clenched her hands at her side. He knew she wanted to slap him for that hateful remark, and he immediately felt contrite. Maybe if he wasn't feeling so defensive, he'd apologize. But he was feeling defensive, and it was easier to blame her.

"You don't know a thing about the circumstances of Melanie's birth." Her voice was calm, belying the heat in her gaze. "Why don't you just thank your lucky stars that I did give her up."

Her hands trembled, and his curiosity heightened.

There was something she wasn't telling him—something important—and he wanted to know. If it meant he had to poke and prod at an obvious open wound to get to the truth, so be it.

"Then why don't you enlighten me," he taunted. "Tell me, Rebecca. Why'd you give her up?"

"Leave it alone, Winslow."

She turned and walked up the steps. He reacted instantly. By the time she reached the door, he was there, reaching over her shoulder to press his hand against the wooden screen door to prevent her escape.

Her sweet scent wrapped around him, and his gut tightened in response. Though she was wearing a pair of faded sweats and a loose fitting T-shirt, she was one of the sexiest women he'd seen in a long time. He wasn't a monk, not by a long shot. But he simply hadn't been interested in the women around Shelbourne.

He leaned closer and inhaled her scent. Why, of all the women he knew, did it have to be Melanie's birth mother that ignited his interest and fired his blood?

"What are you hiding?" he asked from behind her.

Rebecca shivered. Sam was too close, physically and otherwise. She couldn't tell him. There were too many people who would be hurt. Careers could, probably would, be ruined. But more important, Melanie could be hurt, and she refused to allow that to happen. Maybe she *was* suffering from what Sam termed latent maternal instincts, because she'd be damned if Melanie would suffer.

She turned around. Big mistake. He was inches from her. His warm breath fanned her face. He smelled of tobacco and man. Her senses went haywire.

"Why won't you tell me?" His voice was a soft, low rumble of sensuality. Sam was dangerous to those she wanted—needed—to protect. Since she was being honest, at least with herself, he was equally dangerous to her.

"There's nothing to tell. I was sixteen. I got pregnant by one of my father's..." She couldn't tell him. She couldn't tell anyone. No one could ever know the truth. Not even her mother had been aware of the identity of the baby's father or the circumstances of Melanie's conception. It was simply too risky.

She looked into Sam's eyes. "My father made the decision for me. End of story."

"I think there's more."

"You have an overactive imagination."

His gaze traveled over her face, resting on her lips. They suddenly felt drier than dust. Self-consciously she moistened them with the tip of her tongue.

He inched closer until the tips of his boots touched the toes of her sneakers. "What are you hiding?" he repeated in that deep, husky, lover-like voice.

"Nothing," she whispered, and turned her face away.

He muttered something that could have been a curse, then dipped his head and nuzzled her neck as if she'd offered him an invitation. She sucked in a rush of breath when his tongue snaked out and danced along her throat. Dear heaven, what was he doing? Okay, so she knew what he was doing, but she wished he'd stop. She couldn't think straight!

Catching her lower lip between her teeth, she bit back a moan when he lightly nipped that sensitive spot below her ear. She lifted her hand and pressed it against the hard-muscled wall of his chest. Her fingers itched to move upward, to wrap around the back of his neck and pull him closer, to see for herself if his lips held that intoxicating mixture of gentleness and demanding lover she imagined.

He pulled back and looked down at her. Blatant desire mingled with restraint in his chocolate eyes. He smiled suddenly, one of those warm, lazy smiles, with just a hint of danger. "I still think you're full of secrets, Rebecca."

A surge of heat pooled within her belly. She had to get away from this man, and fast, before she made a monumental mistake and flung herself against him—or worse, blurted out the truth. "Good night, Sam," she said, hoping her voice wasn't as shaky as it sounded.

She sidestepped him and gave the door a tug. Thankfully, he released the screen, and she slipped through, wondering how on earth she was going to get through the next few weeks.

Becoming attracted to Sam Winslow was definitely not in her plans. And her life *always* went as planned—until now.

Chapter Five

At least Sam had a normal coffeemaker, Rebecca thought the next morning as she filled the carafe with water. She located the grounds, filled the basket and flipped the switch. Soon the sunny kitchen was filled with the tantalizing aroma of fresh-brewed coffee.

She heard running water, and assumed Sam was in the shower. Just the thought of his powerful body under the spray, with rivulets of steaming water running over his massive chest and down his lean stomach, was enough to shift her hormones into overdrive. She quickly quashed those thoughts, knowing they could only bring about more trouble. She had to stop thinking about Sam Winslow and the way he'd jump-started her feminine senses last night. The man hadn't even kissed her, but she would be a liar if she said she hadn't wanted him to. That realization alone was enough to keep her tossing and turning half the night.

Needing something to do to take her mind off Sam's lips and the way they'd felt pressed against her skin, she attempted to create an edible breakfast. If she concentrated, she could produce passable scrambled eggs and toast. Not much of a meal for a man Sam's size, but it was the best her limited talents would allow.

By the time he joined her twenty minutes later, she was just setting a heaping plate of scrambled eggs on the table along with some toast. She'd discovered ham in the refrigerator, and had warmed a few slices in the oven. A gourmet she was not, but she'd managed to fake it pretty well.

He sat at the table. "Smells good," he said, but she didn't miss the caution lacing his deep, sexy voice.

Not trusting her voice, she just smiled and set a mug of coffee in front of him. She pretended to ignore the way the plain white T-shirt outlined his chest and clung to his biceps. He scooped some eggs onto his plate, added a thick slice of ham, then tentatively tasted the eggs. When his eyes lit up with surprise and appreciation, she tried hard not to let her smile widen, and failed miserably.

She sat across from him and watched him eat while she picked at her own breakfast. Maybe it was the cooking that drove his wife away, she silently quipped. Sam certainly had a healthy appetite. The poor woman must have spent all of her time in the kitchen.

As if he felt her gaze on him, he lifted his eyes to her. He paused with the mug at his lips, his gaze questioning over the rim.

"Why did your marriage end?" she asked suddenly. So much for tact and diplomacy, she thought. Right to the point—that was her motto.

He shrugged. "Christina hated it here."

She set her fork aside. "Here? As in Shelbourne?" *Or here, with you?* She had a hard time believing the latter.

He took another bite of ham and eggs before answering her. "Christina had difficulty adapting to the role of wife to a simple farmer."

"Oh." She sipped her coffee, not knowing what to make out of that statement. He made it sound like farming was something to be ashamed of, and from the size of the Winslow farmstead, *simple* was at the opposite end of the spectrum. After their initial "let's make up a believable story" session during their dinner the previous evening, she'd questioned him on the size of his spread. She'd been surprised to learn that Winslow Wheat & Grain consisted of thousands of acres of rich North Dakota farmland. Although from what she'd seen and heard from the local newscasts, difficulties were not uncommon in a life of farming. One bad year, caused by a slow growing season, drought, or even heavy rains or hail could destroy a crop, and a family. Had Sam suffered a bad year? Had Christina been the type of woman to run at the first sign of trouble? From what little she knew about his ex-wife, it was entirely possible.

She sipped her coffee while Sam reached for another helping of ham and eggs. There was a possibility that Mel was as spoiled as her adopted mother, and she couldn't keep herself from wondering how much of Christina's influence had shaped Mel. If Melanie Winslow understood the lengths her father had gone for her, would she appreciate his efforts or expect them as her due? Only time would tell, and that time was drawing near.

Finished with his breakfast, Sam pushed away from the table and carried his empty plate to the sink, primarily to gain some distance from Rebecca and her questions about past failures. First Mel, and now Rebecca, had forced him to think about things he'd rather not remember. The painful memories of his marriage. And what the breakup had done to his daughter. Mel had cried for her ''mommy'' for days. He'd felt helpless, because Mel's tears had done what Christina's leaving hadn't—broken his heart.

He set the plate in the sink, then refilled his mug with more coffee. It had been a long time since he'd awakened to the scent of freshly brewed coffee or even a breakfast he didn't have to cook himself. The fact that he could easily get used to someone else pulling KP unsettled him. It'd been him and Mel for so long, he'd expected to feel a little more territorial about a stranger making use of his kitchen and was surprised that he didn't mind in the least.

''The men will be in the wheat fields today. I'm driving out with Jake to test some of the crops,'' he said. ''I'm not sure when I'll be back.''

She shrugged, just a gentle lift of one slender

shoulder. He'd thought about that shoulder, the feel, the texture beneath his fingers, along with the taste of her skin and a helluva lot more, all night long.

She rose and began to clear the table. "Does your ex-wife spend time with Melanie?" she asked, bending over to retrieve the empty platter. A pair of cream-colored leggings clung to legs that went on forever. A burgundy thigh-skimming shirt barely covered her very feminine posterior. He nearly groaned at the sight.

He dragged his gaze away from temptation and turned to the kitchen window. Jake stood under the cottonwood organizing the men. A small crew was already in the fields swathing the wheat before the combines came through later. By midafternoon, he hoped to have a few more truckloads of grain delivered to the elevator and the rest placed in grain bins for storage.

"Sam?"

He turned around. She stood at his side, holding the empty dishes in her slender hands.

"I'm sorry, what did you say?"

"Does Melanie spend time with her mother?"

The question seemed odd coming from her. "Mel hasn't seen her mo—" That wasn't right, he thought. Rebecca was Mel's mother, at least biologically. But a mother comforted, guided and protected her child. Rebecca had done none of that. She'd conceived, delivered, then given her child away. But Christina had wanted, complained, then walked away. He'd been the one to sit for hours holding Melanie in a steaming bathroom when she had the croup. He'd been the one to take her to her first day of school. And he'd been the one to hold her when she cried out in the middle of the night once the only mother she ever knew turned her back on her.

"She hasn't seen Christina in eight years," he finally said.

Rebecca stared at him, complete surprise encompassing her delicate features. "Not once?"

"No," he admitted, stepping around her. He strode toward the back door, then stopped and looked over his shoulder. What was it about Rebecca Martinson that made him feel so twisted up inside. He didn't want her here. Her presence was a danger to Mel and to himself, if the thoughts that had kept him awake all night were any indication. So why didn't he just tell her all bets were off and send her packing back to her life in Los Angeles? There wasn't a damn thing she could do about it if he did, either.

So what was stopping him?

After a moment's pause he shook his head and went outside to join Jake, no closer to an answer than he'd been at 3:00 a.m.

REBECCA WATCHED SAM through the kitchen window as he crossed the yard toward the cottonwood trees where the men in his employ had gathered with Jake. She'd hesitated to ask about his ex-wife, primarily because she suspected she would hit a hot button or two. Instead Sam had surprised her once again by responding to her questions.

Convinced she'd never understand her daughter's father, she grabbed a damp dishcloth and started wiping down the counters until she heard the squeak of the back door opening.

"Sam?"

When he didn't answer, she turned. A curvy, petite woman with russet hair and eyes as blue as cornflowers stood staring at her, a casserole dish in her delicate hands and surprise in her eyes.

Rebecca managed a smile. "Hi."

"And who might you be?" she asked congenially, stepping more fully into the kitchen.

"Rebecca Martinson. Sam and I are..." What? This woman obviously didn't know who she was.

"Oh, you must be Sammy's friend. He mentioned you were coming for a visit." The other woman grinned and set her casserole on the table. "I'm Carrie Harrison."

"It's a pleasure, Ms. Harrison."

"Carrie," she corrected. "Is Sammy in the fields?"

Sammy, huh?

"He just left," Rebecca answered, stifling a grin.

Sammy?

The back door squeaked again, and Sam strode back into the kitchen. The dark look on his face told Rebecca his earlier good mood had evaporated in the ten minutes he'd been gone.

"Sam, honey, I brought you a hot dish for dinner.

I figured you'd be busy in the fields, and with Mel gone and all..." Carrie shrugged her slim shoulders and approached Sam. She raised on tiptoe and placed a kiss on his freshly shaved cheek.

Rebecca lifted a brow at Sam. Looked like little Miss Curvy Harrison was on real friendly terms with the local plowboy.

Sam nearly groaned. He appreciated Carrie's efforts, but he could have done without the theatrics, which he was certain were for Rebecca's benefit. He didn't need this, not now with the crops ready to come in and Mel due to arrive home in a few days.

He looked at Rebecca, who quietly went about his kitchen as if she belonged there, putting things away as though she'd been doing it for years. He tried to massage away the tension bunching the muscles in his neck.

"I know it's a bad time, Sammy," Carrie said, "but I'm having a little trouble with that milking machine again. Do you think you could come over and take a look at it for me?"

"I'll see if Jake can get away a little later today," he said, his gaze following Rebecca and the gentle sway of her hips. She ignored him, and Carrie, as she walked into the pantry. She stood on tiptoe in the pantry placing things on the shelf, her shirt inching up over her delectable bottom again. He couldn't help himself, he followed the length of her legs down to her toes and back up again, over her backside and...

"I'd appreciate it." Carrie sighed, a wistful sound that suddenly irritated him.

"You know, Sammy, I've been thinking." Carrie laid a hand possessively on his arm—again he was certain to let Rebecca know that she'd staked her claim. "You need someone who can take meals out to the fields. I'd be more than willing to help out."

Yeah, he'd just bet she would. Carrie Harrison had been chasing after him since Christina left, but lately her tactics had become more brazen.

"We'll make do, Carrie," he told her firmly, reminding himself he needed to hire someone and quick. The last thing he needed was Carrie hanging around his house, cooking for him and Mel and the hands. He'd done the neighborly thing and helped repair her barn a few months ago. Ever since then, she kept finding excuses to call him and ask for his help. And she'd made it more than clear how she wanted to repay him.

Rebecca stepped out of the pantry, knowing she should have her head examined for even thinking about what she was planning to do. Sam had already agreed to let her stay the month. It wasn't as if she needed to make herself indispensable. But she was grateful for the time he'd granted her. The least she could do was pitch in while she was here, even if she had no idea what "pitching in" might mean.

She took a deep breath. "Thank you for your offer, Ms. Harrison, but that's part of the reason I'm here."

Sam and Carrie both turned to stare at her. Sam

looked at her as if she'd grown two heads. Carrie looked as if she wanted to decapitate her.

"A decent meal is one of my...talents," she lied and flashed Sam her sultriest grin. Okay, so she was being stupid and petty. It wasn't like she was jealous or anything.

Sam's narrowed gaze held a wealth of skepticism. He was probably remembering the ruined skillet and that horrid salad dressing from last night.

"I've hosted plenty of dinner parties in my day." Of course, all the arrangements were made by party planners and caterers. But how difficult could it be? She'd managed a respectable breakfast, hadn't she? And she'd even picked out all the eggshells that had fallen into the mix.

Carrie glared at her, then quicker than a blink cast a pretty smile up at Sam. "Well, the offer is there if you need it," she said, her doubtfulness more than apparent. "I'd better be going."

Rebecca smiled at Sam. "It'll give me something to do," she said once Carrie left. "I'd really like to help out."

"Are you sure you know what you're doing?" Sam asked. "Have you ever cooked for a couple dozen men. *Hungry* men?"

"How hard can it be?" The bright smile she flashed didn't waver one iota as she wondered what had possessed her to do something so incredibly as-inine. Unfortunately, she had a pretty good idea. Either those masochistic tendencies were rearing their heads again, or the minute Carrie batted her corn-flower-blues at Sam the green-eyed monster she never realized she'd been acquainted with charged into action.

"This means dinner and supper. Two meals," he said holding up as many fingers. "Every single day. Monday through Saturday, and sometimes on Sunday."

"No problem," she said with a carefree wave of her hand.

"You're sure?"

"Absolutely," she told him. "It'll be no problem whatsoever."

No problem at all, she thought, when Sam left through the back door again, grumbling something about men, mutiny and unpredictable women.

Really, she thought, heading into the study in search of the telephone book. How hard could it be to hire a caterer?

MEAL PREPARATION was the least of Rebecca's problems. Locating a caterer had taken more effort and money than she'd dreamed, but after numerous telephone calls she'd finally commissioned the diner in Shelbourne. She'd even managed to get enough pre-cooked meals she could freeze for Sundays. All she had to do was thaw, warm and serve, and no one, particularly one skeptical landowner, would be the wiser.

But, it turned out there was more than just cooking

she needed to worry about. Last night when Sam had innocently asked her if he had any clean T-shirts, she'd nearly fallen over in surprise. Cooking *and* housework? She'd assumed all she'd have to worry about were meals. There hadn't been a single word whispered about taking care of the house, as well, until he'd explained how his mother had handled the chores prior to relocating to Arizona.

She *definitely* needed to get her head examined. She had to have a chemical imbalance that made her *volunteer* for this duty, she thought as she sprinkled scouring powder in the bathtub.

She bent over the tub and scrubbed. If she lost her license to practice law, one thing was certain—she'd never survive as a maid. Housework was most definitely not her forte.

With a sigh, she tossed the scrub brush into the bucket. Bending over the tub again, she turned on the faucet, but the water wouldn't reach the rear to rinse away the scouring powder. Sighing again, she tugged the knob for the shower, hoping the spray would wash the powder down the drain. Looking over her shoulder toward the rear of the tub, she waited for the water.

Nothing!

"Come on," she muttered, and tugged harder on the knob. The pipes shook and groaned. Still no water.

Leaving the knob on the open position, she looked

up at the showerhead. Had she bumped or moved something when cleaning? she wondered.

Without warning, the showerhead rattled as if possessed. Icy cold water spurted out, drenching her in a matter of seconds.

Sam's laughter floated over her, and she turned to give him a heated glare. Of all the times he would pick to walk in on her, this had to be it. "I'm glad one of us finds this situation humorous, Winslow."

"I'm sorry," he laughed, pulling a towel from the rack and handing it to her. "I should have warned you. No one really uses this bathroom. The shower doesn't always work right, and I haven't had a chance to call in a plumber."

"Dad?"

Rebecca froze. Oh, God, this was it.

Sam visibly stiffened.

"Dad, who are you…" a girl's voice called from the hallway.

Melanie stepped into the spacious bathroom. Rebecca swallowed hard. Oh, God. She fought a battle of personal restraint. Gathering Melanie in her arms and holding her tight was not the way to do things. To Melanie she was a stranger. Yet, the driving need to announce who she really was shocked her. As much as she told Sam she had no intention of revealing her identity, that was exactly what she wanted to do.

She hadn't realized Sam had even gone to bring Melanie home. He hadn't said a word when he left the house after breakfast, and she'd just assumed they would go together—this evening when the men had finished plowing or whatever it was they did all day.

She wanted to make a good impression. She wanted Melanie to like her—she wanted them to become friends. She wanted…so much she couldn't keep it all straight any longer. But she certainly didn't want to meet Melanie for the first time looking like a scullery maid.

"Hi," Melanie said, and looked from her to Sam.

Sam cleared his throat. "Mel. This is Rebecca Martinson. We're old friends."

A lump the size of the Los Angeles Coliseum clogged Rebecca's throat. She blinked back a rush of tears. She couldn't cry—not now, no matter how much she wanted to. She'd cried when she'd had to give Melanie up, great heart-wrenching sobs, and she feared they'd pour from her again. With sudden clarity she realized the pain she'd kept hidden over the years hadn't eased. No. The pain had merely been pushed to the background, forsaken, but never forgotten. What she really feared was opening the floodgate and turning loose the emptiness of the last fourteen years.

"I was just…uh…cleaning up," she finally said. No one would ever believe she stood before the courts arguing cases, changing tactics without a moment's hesitation. Not when she couldn't find the words to form a decent greeting.

"Rebecca offered to spend her vacation with us

and help out," Sam offered, his tone gruff. "Until I can hire someone."

She just stood there, a puddle of water gathering around her sneakers, her red T-shirt plastered against her chest and dripping all over her jeans, staring at her daughter. She'd waited fourteen years for this moment, and she didn't have a clue what to say or how to begin to form a friendship, because that's all she could ever have, *with her own daughter!*

She silently cursed her father for railroading a seventeen-year-old girl into believing that giving up her child was the only choice available to her. And she cursed Sam for making her promise she wanted nothing more than to meet that child. A promise she had to keep, and one that would cost her more heartache and pain.

"It's nice to meet you." Melanie smiled, then turned her attention back to Sam. "Where's Dutch?"

Sam looked down at his daughter, a few of his fears slipping away. On the drive home from the hospital, he'd worried there might be some mystical connection between Rebecca and Mel, that the moment Mel laid eyes on Rebecca she'd know she was her birth mother. But, Mel was more interested in her dog than the strange woman standing in his bathroom looking like a drowned rat. An adorable drowned rat.

Turning his gaze back to Rebecca, he couldn't help noticing how the wet T-shirt clung to and outlined very full breasts. Even with her hair pulled up in a ponytail, and little or no makeup, she was sexy as hell.

"Dad?" Mel tugged on his sleeve. "Dutch?" She asked again in an exasperated tone.

With effort, Sam pulled his gaze from Rebecca. "He's been sleeping in the barn with Cheyenne. He was moping around the house, so I booted him out."

"Dutch isn't used to sleeping outside!"

"He hasn't been outside," he corrected. "He's been in the barn."

"Same difference," Melanie said, crossing her arms over her chest and giving him an indignant stare that reminded him all too much of Rebecca.

"Who's Dutch?" Rebecca asked in a tight voice with a shaky-at-best smile.

"He's my dog." Mel grinned at her then turned to him, that haughty look back in her eyes. "And *you* threw him out of the house."

"I didn't *throw* him out. He was lying around in your room all the time. I thought…"

"You probably hurt his feelings."

"I doubt that," he grumbled. Why were they discussing the brooding temperament of a lazy Labrador? Wasn't Mel the least bit curious why a strange woman was in their home?

Mel shook her head and rolled her eyes.

Apparently not.

"If you'll excuse me, I'd like to change into something a little drier," Rebecca said. "The men will be expecting supper soon."

"Sure." Sam backed out of the bathroom, taking Mel with him.

He watched Rebecca hurry down the hall toward her bedroom as if she couldn't wait to gain some distance. He'd give anything to know what she was thinking right now.

Mel leaned close to him, wrapped her arms around his middle, and gave him a gentle squeeze. "Who is she?"

He laid his arm over her shoulders and held her close. God, she'd grown up so much in the past couple of years. He knew it was only a matter of time before she'd leave home to lead her own life. But he had a few years left with her, thanks to Rebecca, and he planned on making the best of that time.

"We were friends in college," he lied. He'd never lied to Mel, and doing so now caused his anger to spark. He blamed Rebecca.

Mel slipped out of his embrace and tugged his hand, leading him toward the staircase. "Why's she here?"

"I told you. She's on vacation." That much, at least, was the truth. "I needed some help with Grandy gone and Rebecca offered."

"She's pretty, Dad."

"Is she? I hadn't noticed."

Mel laughed. "Right, Dad. Is she your girlfriend?"

"No. We're just—"

"Old friends," she finished for him, leading him

toward the back door. "She could be your girl-friend."

"Mel," he warned. He knew where this conversation was going and that was not a path he planned to travel. He couldn't deny that Rebecca fired his blood, any more than he could deny he thought about her at odd times the past few days. But it was a case of pure-and-simple lust. And he'd never admit *that* to his daughter.

"Let's go find Dutch. He's gonna be mad at you, so you're gonna have to kiss up to him."

"I will not 'kiss up' to that lazy, piece of—"

"Dad!"

He shrugged and let his daughter lead him out of the house. She could lead him anywhere she wanted and he'd follow, now that she was home where she belonged.

With him—and her birth mother.

Chapter Six

"How is she?"

Sam glanced up from the journal entries he'd been making to find Rebecca standing in the doorway to his office, a wicker laundry basket tucked beneath her arm. He'd never in a millennium dreamed the elegant attorney he'd approached a few days ago to save his daughter's life would be folding his jockey shorts, but he did appreciate her help since he still hadn't gotten around to placing an ad for a housekeeper and cook. He made a mental note to take care of it tomorrow. The last thing he wanted to do was depend on Rebecca. She might enjoy playing house now, but he knew from experience that women like her just weren't cut out for life on the farm. Besides, in three weeks she'd return to Los Angeles and be out of their lives.

What was he even doing, thinking about playing house with her?

Because you want her, Winslow.

"She's tiring easily, but that's to be expected." He

dropped his pen on the desk and leaned back, stretching his arms over his head, ignoring the nagging voice in his mind and the corresponding stir of his groin. "I have a feeling keeping her quiet for any length of time is going to take some effort."

She stepped into the office, set the basket on the floor and perched on the arm of the brown leather sofa, the bright late-afternoon sunlight shining through the window behind her. Soft, faded jeans clung to legs that fueled his fantasies. The clinging wet T-shirt that had outlined things he had no businesses thinking about had been replaced with a soft, white cotton, button-down shirt.

Three weeks. You can contain your lust for this woman for three weeks.

"She's so beautiful," Rebecca said, her eyes filled with an emotion Sam didn't want to name. An emotion that could lead to hurt and disillusionment. An emotion that leaped from curiosity about the child she gave away, clear to something much more maternal…and dangerous.

"Thank you," he said automatically, in spite of how ridiculous the response made him feel. Mel didn't get her looks from him. The person responsible, at least partially, was the woman in front of him. "I meant—"

"No, it's okay." She stood suddenly and paced in front of his desk. "I didn't realize how awkward this would be."

And things would get more awkward if he acted on the ridiculous fantasies haunting him.

The phone on his desk jangled and he reached for it, glad he didn't have to comment on her last statement. "Hello?"

"Let me speak to Rebecca Martinson," a deep, rich baritone demanded.

Sam looked over at Rebecca as she turned to pace in front of his desk again, a worried frown marring her features. "Who's calling?" he asked, enjoying the gentle sway of her hips as she continued to pace.

"Justice Martinson."

"Hold on." He punched the button on the cordless phone. "It's for you. Your father."

Her frown deepened, but the look she cast his way was filled with apprehension and, he thought, a trace of fear. She took the phone from him and turned toward the window overlooking the front lawn. "Yes?"

The formality of her response surprised him. *My father made the decision for me.* On second thought, perhaps not.

Rebecca stiffened, waiting for her father's tirade. He'd tracked her down, a fact that irritated her and would no doubt add to his ire. Once he learned the truth of her whereabouts, she suspected he'd be furious with her. Anger and displeasure were the two emotions she'd developed quite a skill for evoking within the almighty Justice Albert Martinson.

"Rebecca? What are you doing in North Dakota?" She held back the sigh on her lips. Not an ounce of concern tinged his voice, only demand. With little effort she imagined eyes so like her own flaring with fury. His salt-and-pepper brows would be pulled into the same ferocious frown that had made her wary as a child, his lips thinned into a straight, disapproving line.

"It's rather complicated," she said pushing the images from her mind. She didn't have to look over her shoulder to know that Sam was still seated behind his desk watching her. "Can I call you back?" *Like in three weeks.*

"No, you cannot," her father barked. "Rebecca, I demand to know what's going on. I've been trying to reach you for days."

She didn't have to ask how he found her. She'd left word with Laura how to reach her in an emergency. Obviously, her father had declared her absence such, and had demanded her secretary inform him of her whereabouts.

"I'm taking some time off work." She opted for evasion, if even for a few moments, to get her thoughts in order. Just one more disappointment, she thought, to add to her list of faults. Another black mark against the rebellious daughter. The battle lines had been drawn years before, there was no reason for her to think that her father might actually support her now.

"Obviously," he replied, his voice dripping with sarcasm.

"I'll go check on Mel," Sam whispered, then quietly slipped out of the room and closed the door to his study. She was grateful for the privacy. While she didn't believe she'd ever be so bold as to actually get into a shouting match with her father, as raw as her emotions were at the moment, anything was possible.

She dropped into the chair Sam vacated and leaned back into the soft leather. The chair, molded to his large, masculine body, was still warm. Briefly she closed her eyes and breathed in the rich scent of worn leather, spice and something uniquely Sam. She opened eyes, strangely comforted and encouraged.

"A few days ago someone came into my office," she told her father. Not just someone—her daughter's father. Sam Winslow, a man who made her curious about things like deep kisses, need and desire, sensations she'd once believed would forever be beyond her. "He's the adoptive parent of my...of my daughter."

She waited, expecting an explosion of temper, followed by a diatribe of the ridiculousness of her actions, concluded with heated demands that she return to California at once and stop this foolishness. She wasn't going to be disappointed.

"What," he said in a low voice seething with anger, "do you think you're doing, Rebecca?"

She leaned her head against the back of the chair and breathed in more of Sam's scent.

"She needed me," she whispered. And maybe, in some ways, she needed Mel as well. "She needed bone marrow and I was a match. I'm taking some time to get to know her.''

''I demand that you come home this instant. Get out of there before you do something even more incredibly stupid than you already have.''

Despite his bluster, despite his demands, she knew she couldn't leave. At least not yet. ''No.''

''No? Rebecca, you know the risks involved.''

True, she did. But she also understood the risks her father was referring to were eons away from those she would willingly suffer. Her heart would never be the same again; she understood that, and still she knew that she'd never fall asleep again each night without thinking about her daughter. The baby that'd been taken away from her was no longer a faceless entity, but a living and breathing young girl who would go through her life never knowing the stranger who came to stay for a month really wasn't the old college pal of her adoptive father's as she'd been led to believe. Oh, Rebecca knew the risks, and she accepted responsibility for each of them because this time she *did* have a choice.

''Yes, I do,'' she finally said, a little shocked by the determination in her voice. ''I know what's at stake.''

''Then come home. Now,'' Justice Martinson demanded again.

''No, Dad. Not this time.''

He let out a sigh. ''People can be hurt, Rebecca,'' he said, attempting to reason with her. ''Do you want to be responsible for damaging the reputation and career of Senator—''

"I know people can be hurt," she interrupted. Would she ever have a conversation with her father that didn't include an argument? She knew the answer to that question, but it didn't mean the ache to mend the rifts between them ceased to exist. "I could be hurt," she said. "My daughter could be hurt."

"That's not what I'm talking about, and you know it."

She stood, feeling edgy, and paced. Anger at her father's callousness brewed beneath the surface. Her entire life had been spent trying to please a man who would never be happy with her. Why couldn't she just accept that and get on with her life and stop worrying what her father thought. She'd lost track of the number of times she'd forgone her own desires to please him, and for what? How foolish she'd been to think she could make him proud of her.

"Oh, I think I know *who* you mean, Dad. Do you really think I'd be silly enough to think you'd care one way or another if I could be hurt? I learned a long time ago that isn't going to happen."

He sighed again, the sound filled with more exasperation. A more common emotion they never shared. "You're being selfish," he told her angrily. "Careers are at stake. Important careers."

"What could be more important than the life of a child?" she asked incredulously.

"Come home, Rebecca," he ordered again, ignoring her question. "Come home now and forget this foolishness."

The line went dead. He'd never understand. He hadn't understood her then. Why had she expected him to do so now? Perhaps because this time she refused to buckle under to the pressure, hoping instead that he'd see her determination as strength rather than rebellion. Which was silly, she thought, setting the cordless phone back on the mount. She hadn't given in when she'd made the decision to practice family law, despite the fact her choice had furthered the wedge between them.

To Justice Martinson it made no difference that she was an excellent lawyer, or even a junior partner in a prestigious Los Angeles firm. Her accomplishments were meaningless for the simple reason she'd dared to defy him.

She let out a sigh and realized the futility of believing her father would ever be proud of her. And, she decided, it was long past the time for her to accept the hurtful truth.

"Nothing."

Rebecca spun around at the sound of Sam's voice. "Excuse me?" She'd been lost in thought and hadn't heard him come into the room.

"Nothing is more important than the life of a child," he said, crossing the room toward her.

"My father feels differently," she said, propping her backside on the edge of the desk. "It's a long-standing Martinson practice for my father and me to be on opposite sides of the fence. We're just keeping up the tradition.''

"I'm sorry. That must be painful," he said, his voice filled with a tenderness that touched a place deep inside her.

She pulled in a deep breath and fought back an unaccustomed rush of tears. She would *not* cry just because her father was too stubborn to take the time to understand his own daughter. She wouldn't cry, she thought, wiping the lone tear escaping down her cheek just because Sam was being kind and understanding.

"Ah, Rebecca," Sam said on a husky rumble. With a gentle tug he pulled her away from the desk and into his arms.

She never once considered refusing the comfort he offered her, and rested her cheek against his firm, wide chest. The heavy rhythm of his heart, combined with the feel of his strong arms sliding around her to hold her close, hinted at something beyond comfort. Something that would lead them both down a path toward disaster.

When she'd first decided to come to Shelbourne, she'd had one thing in mind; get acquainted with her daughter. She understood the potential heartache and had accepted it as her due. The one thing she hadn't planned on was a wild case of desire for Sam Winslow.

She lifted her head and looked into his eyes. Desire mirrored desire. Whatever their problems, whatever their differences, this jurisdiction was crystal clear—need.

Her heart beat just a little faster as she snuggled closer, lifting her lips toward his until they were a breath away from touching. He muttered something that failed to penetrate the sensual fog weaving through her mind, but he accepted her invitation and brought their lips together just the same.

The first brush of his mouth against hers was gentle, almost tentative. The second was more in line with the images that had kept her tossing and turning all week.

He shifted their bodies and pulled her flush against him, deepening the kiss, taking the sensual exploration to the next level.

She made a little sound in the back of her throat, somewhere between a whimper and a moan, giving in to electrifying currents sparking through her veins.

His hand on her hip rocked her closer, holding her against him and making no attempt to hide his arousal. The deep ache inside her intensified with sweet anticipation. She wanted Sam so much. Wanted him like she hadn't wanted another man in a very long time. The wanting was as foreign to her as the simmering sensation low in her belly and spreading outward with liquid warmth.

After her divorce, she'd concentrated on her career, and there just hadn't been time to cultivate a relationship. She'd told herself the sacrifices she'd made for her career were worth the twelve- to fourteen-hour days at the office. As Sam's tongue swept across hers with the skill of a practiced lover, she acknowledged she hadn't sacrificed anything, but had used her career as an excuse to avoid intimacy.

Oh, sweet heaven, if Sam made love with a fraction of the skill he kissed, avoidance would be the last thing she wanted to practice.

Her father had accused her of being foolish. Now she *was* definitely behaving foolishly. She had no business even considering making love to Sam Winslow. More than eighteen hundred miles separated them. A lifetime of choices and circumstances stood between them.

Reluctantly she eased out of his arms. He released her, but she felt his unwillingness to let her go. The truth had her heart skipping a beat.

"This isn't right," she said, her voice barely above a whisper. She had no idea whether she meant their hotter-than-the-North-Dakota-sun kiss or the realization that she hadn't felt an ounce of fear in his arms.

"It felt damned right to me," he said in a ragged voice, his tone filled with more than a hint of the sexual frustration she was feeling.

She pulled in a deep breath. "That was pretty darned fantastic, Winslow," she said, aiming for sassy, but the trembling in her voice had her falling short of her goal.

"But?" he said, his dark brows pulling into a frown.

"*But* you know as well as I do we'd be making a

huge mistake,'' she said regretfully, then scooped up the laundry basket and hurried out of the room, putting as much distance between herself and temptation as possible.

REBECCA SET ASIDE the legal thriller she'd been attempting to read for the past couple of hours, next to the clock on the bedside table. It was a few minutes after nine, yet despite the late hour the sun wouldn't set for close to two hours. She felt restless and edgy and unable to concentrate. The idea of hiding out in her room until she finally fell asleep held no appeal, especially since that wouldn't be for at least another four hours or more. Even though she'd been in the Midwest for a week, her internal clock continued to keep Pacific time. While the time was really just past nine, her body said seven. She rarely left the office before seven in the evenings, or went to sleep before midnight. The thought of even trying now was almost enough to send her from her room.

Funny, she thought, swinging her feet to the floor. She never figured herself for the type to run away from anything, but hiding out in her room spoke volumes. She *was* hiding. Not from Sam or even from the newly awakened desire he'd stirred inside her. No, she was hiding from herself. From her past. A past she'd worked so very hard to overcome.

She crossed the room to the window. Maybe she hadn't really overcome anything. Pushing aside the sheer curtains to gaze down at the yard below, she attempted to ignore the truth, but her own personality quirks refused to allow her that luxury. The truth was that all she'd managed to do was bury the past fifteen years. Following in the Martinson tradition, stoic silence had been her talisman. She understood that by playing mind games with herself, by refusing to speak of the past, she had believed it could not possibly hurt her. If she didn't think of the past, then it couldn't sneak up on her when she least expected it. If she pretended the pain didn't exist, then there'd be nothing to haunt her or influence her decisions in the present.

All the tools she'd used to cope, survive and live through the past fifteen years had lost their effectiveness the minute Sam Winslow had walked into her life. His presence meant that she could no longer keep the memories behind the barred doors of her mind. Because he'd come into her life, the memories had seeped past the barriers and moved out of the darkness into the shadows, not quite moving directly into the light for all to examine and prod like a lab experiment gone bad. Instead, they were there only for her to see, to feel and, dammit, to remember.

She didn't blame the kiss she shared with Sam for turning those memories loose in her mind. No, that was an honor, she thought sarcastically, reserved for the great Justice Martinson. His callous ideas of parenting had jarred loose what she'd kept hidden for too long.

She gripped the sheers, twisting the chiffon like

fabric around her fingers. Her father had blamed her then, just as he blamed her now for the choices she'd made. Nothing would ever change between them. He continued to punish her by issuing edicts and demands and expressing his disappointment in her when she refused to heed his warnings. No matter how unfair his actions had been and continued to be, no matter how much she'd never stopped wanting otherwise, her father would always lay the blame for what happened that day in the gazebo during her seventeenth birthday party at her feet.

And just as she'd never stopped wanting otherwise, anger continued to simmer within her.

A sound, briefly reminiscent of laughter, although far too caustic to be filled with humor, escaped her. Some things never changed, and her relationship with her father was one of them.

A noise from below caught her attention, and she let the sheers slip from her fingers to flutter back into place. Sam stepped out from beneath the shade of a cottonwood tree, his gaze turned upward, toward her window.

She took a step back, but continued to watch the man who ignited her passion just as easily as he struck the match to light his nightly vice. Getting involved with Sam was nothing short of plain stupid. No matter how much she twisted the idea around, she came up with the same answer every single time—heartbreak.

She sighed and turned away from the window.

Something struck the screen, then again, until she returned to the window. Sam tossed something in the air, caught it in his large hand, then tossed it up in the air again. "You gonna hide behind those curtains all night, Counselor?"

How could someone she barely knew understand her so well?

She let out a sigh and brushed the curtain aside. Leaning down, she braced both arms on the sill. "Didn't your mama teach you not to throw stones?"

"That only applies to people who live in glass houses," he called up to her. "You gonna stay up there all night?"

"I don't know," she said, then glanced over her shoulder. "I'm kinda getting used to my little ivory tower."

"Isn't it lonely in your tower?"

She slowly shook her head. "I've got plenty of company." With all of her resurrected memories, how could she possibly be lonely?

"Mel wants to watch a movie and was asking for you."

From what she'd learned about Sam the past few days, she knew he wasn't the kind of man to run or hide from his problems. Sam faced challenges head-on. His coming to her office was a perfect example, as was his agreeing to her spending a month at the farm. Regardless of the fears he must be harboring about her and wondering if her motivations were as honest as she claimed them to be, he'd tackled his insecurities. His invitation to her to join them now was a perfect example.

She'd only managed to feed her own insecurities and fears by bolting out of the study after that electrifying kiss.

"You sure you don't mind?" she asked him.

He shot a glance toward the back door then looked back up at her. "I thought you came here to spend some time with her?" he asked, lowering his deep voice.

So did she, but now that Melanie was home, Rebecca found herself feeling even more insecure than she'd ever dreamed possible. It wasn't that she didn't know what to say to Melanie, but she feared she might say something that would give her away. Sam was right, Melanie wasn't stupid. Rebecca saw the physical similarities between them. Wouldn't her daughter eventually see them, as well?

She had two choices. Either continue to hide out in her room or join Sam and Melanie and pretend she and Sam were nothing more than old friends.

"I'll be right down," she told him, opting for the latter.

People can be hurt, Rebecca.

Her father's words rang in her ear as she left the sanctity of her bedroom. For the first time in a very long time, she agreed with her father, even if they were referring to different people.

Chapter Seven

Sam adjusted the armful of clothes Mel had been having him hold for the past thirty minutes and rocked back on his heels. He felt as if he was watching from a distance rather than playing an active role in the scene as Mel and Rebecca searched the racks in the department store for the latest fashions suitable for a teenager. Bitterness and resentment pushed their way to the surface. He tried to force those emotions down but glared at Rebecca instead. He'd been shopping for his daughter himself for years without the assistance of a woman. There wasn't much about a little girl's apparel he didn't know, from lacy socks to the latest blue jean craze. Hell, he'd even taken Mel to buy her first bra last year and, to his credit, hadn't made a single blunder to embarrass her. Watching Mel practically blossom under Rebecca's expert fashion sense made him feel like an interloper.

Mel held up a red sweater with a crest-like emblem on the front for Rebecca's inspection. She shook her head and handed Mel a hunter-green with cream rugby stripes instead. Mel snagged the sweater and paired it with the cream-colored pants in her hand. "Here, Dad. Hold these," she said, shoving the garments at him, then turning back to her mother.

"How much more do you plan on buying, Mel?" he asked, readjusting his already overburdened arms.

She grinned and shrugged. "We've only picked out four outfits."

We? Somehow he didn't think *he* was a part of that *we*. He really shouldn't be jealous about all the time mother and daughter were spending together, or that Mel had completely disregarded his opinion and taken Rebecca's advice over his since they'd started this shopping expedition. He really shouldn't feel threatened by the easy friendship that had been forged between mother and daughter. Yet, knowing those things didn't alleviate the twist to his heart every time Mel hung on every word Rebecca spoke or took her advice, disregarding his own. He tried to tell himself his feelings were based on the fear that Mel could learn the truth and be hurt because he'd lied to her about Rebecca's identity, but he sensed his feelings went far deeper. Rebecca was a threat to his relationship with Mel. And if he wasn't careful, he could end up alienating his daughter.

Since Mel had come home from the hospital, he'd been trying to get caught up with all the paperwork that had piled up over the past weeks, leaving her alone for long hours with Rebecca. It was no wonder they'd become friends, he thought, and blamed himself. Running a farming operation the size of Winslow Wheat & Grain took a great deal of time and concentration. The paperwork alone was mountainous.

A part of him longed for the days he'd been able to work in the fields alongside the few men he'd once employed during the planting and harvesting seasons. He missed the physical aspects, but decided the lack of physical labor was a small price to pay for turning the once-simple farmstead into the successful operation it was today. Now he employed more than a half dozen men year-round and hired dozens more during harvest. He'd invested wisely over the years, purchasing more and more land and even adding a small cattle operation. His workload had grown with the added responsibilities, and meetings with accountants, lawyers and other industry professionals kept him away from what he loved most—the land.

When Mel suggested the three of them go shopping for school clothes, he'd thought getting out of the house for a while and spending time with his daughter was a great idea. What he really wanted to do, and what he'd never admit to Mel, was to hit the fields with the men and just work until he was too exhausted to think or dream about a dark-haired, emerald-eyed woman with a sassy mouth that tasted sweeter than the finest wine.

Rebecca laughed at something Mel said, a sweet, husky sound that tightened his gut. Five days had passed since he'd kissed her, and although he'd tried to keep his distance from her physically, he couldn't stop thinking about her. How he'd wanted her, and he still did, with astonishing intensity. Thank goodness at least one of them had come to their senses. If she hadn't pulled away, he couldn't help wondering just how far they might have gone. His body had been primed and ready, and he suspected hers had been, as well. He'd even tried to keep his distance, but with her living under his roof, the issue was a moot point. So was dousing the flame simmering inside him whenever she crept into his thoughts.

He shifted his position again and watched mother and daughter deep in conversation over a rack filled with dresses. The similarities between them were amazing, some blatant, others more subtle. Rebecca used her hands when she spoke. So did Mel. Mel tapped her index finger against her lips when she concentrated on something. So did Rebecca. But there were differences as well. Where Mel was open, Rebecca was reserved. And she was a woman with a secret.

He frowned. Her secrets were none of his business. She may have saved his tail with the men by pitching in, but he wasn't a fool and knew she'd hired the Shelbourne Diner. Other than the few years he'd spent in college, he'd lived his entire life in Shelbourne. No one within a fifty-mile radius made fried chicken with country gravy and biscuits the way Wilma Parker did.

While he admired Rebecca's resourcefulness, he wasn't all that surprised. Women like her just weren't cut out for the simple life. Her background, social standing and the advantages she'd been afforded separated her. She might enjoy the role she was playing for now, but year after year of isolation with nothing glamorous or exciting to detract from the day-to-day drudgery of life on the farm would make her bitter and resentful, just like Christina.

He wasn't a chauvinist, not by a long shot, but he understood some women preferred a life of domesticity to that of Corporate America or the Social Registry. Just because Rebecca had sewn a few buttons on his shirts or learned how to dump the right ingredients into the bread machine didn't mean she was planning to exchange her power suits for an apron. And just because he'd spent an evening or two with her and enjoyed himself more than was prudent didn't mean a thing. In a little more than two weeks, she would leave, and his and Mel's life would return to normal.

He hoped.

"Would those lacy type of panty hose look right with this or the ribbed kind?"

Panty hose? Mel's question jarred him back to reality. Mel was too young to start thinking in terms of panty hose. "Wait a minute," he said, causing both women to look at him curiously. "You're not old enough for that kind of stuff yet."

"Dad, I need a couple of dresses this year," Mel said, holding up a paisley dress with a black velvet Peter Pan collar. "I am in high school now, you know."

Yes, he knew. He knew his daughter was growing up way too fast to suit him, too. That she was even considering wearing dresses only reinforced that little fact of life.

"I was thinking a pair of low-heeled boots would look nice," Rebecca offered by way of compromise. "The ones that lace up the front."

"You'll freeze wearing that thing," Sam said, thinking of the cold winter days ahead.

Mel sighed, a heavy dramatic sound and rolled her eyes. "I'm going to try this on," she said, and disappeared into the dressing room.

Rebecca hid a smile at Sam's fierce scowl. Growing pains, she decided. His, not Melanie's.

She turned back to the display piled with sweaters and found a pale-pink one with soft-green and yellow flecks, but didn't feel the color was right for Mel's dramatic coloring. She reached for a raspberry mock turtleneck and another in royal purple with a delicate teal-and-gold-plaid design that would look adorable with the short teal skirt Mel had liked.

She felt him come up behind her and lean in close. "What are you doing?" he asked, his tone low and soft.

She glanced over her shoulder at him. The look in his eyes was anything but soft. "Melanie picked out a couple of skirts and I'm trying to find sweaters to match." She turned her attention back to a handmade navy-blue knit vest that would look great with a denim skirt and simple white blouse.

"That's not what I meant."

Oh, she knew exactly what he meant. He referred to her accepting Mel's invitation to help the girl select clothes for the upcoming school year. The shopping trip had coincided with a medical checkup, and as much as she'd known Sam had wanted otherwise, when Melanie had asked her to come along, she wasn't about to refuse. She needed all the memories she could collect to treasure later, because according to Sam, that's all she would have in the years to come.

She breathed in, adding his own spicy scent mingled with the aroma of man to her collection of memories. Her insides fluttered despite the fact she'd sworn she was *not* attracted to Sam Winslow. She'd practically forgotten all about the kiss they'd shared in his study. It had meant nothing. She'd been feeling sorry for herself, and Sam had offered comfort. Just because he'd set her soul on fire and made her wish for things that could never be didn't mean a thing.

She sighed. The only problem with her argument was that she'd never been a very good liar, even to herself.

"I'm not talking about the clothes," he added in a harsh whisper. "You're trying to fit in, and I want you to knock it off."

"I don't know what you're talking about." She moved away to the rack with blouses. They'd spotted a white oxford button-down earlier that would work well with the knit vest.

"Oh, I think you do," he said, following close behind. "You'll only be here a little more than two weeks, but once you leave for L.A., Rebecca, it's over. It has to be. For all our sakes."

She bit back the sharp reply hovering on her lips as Mel stepped out of the dressing room to model the dress. Rebecca didn't want her time with Melanie to end, and she resented the reminder. Even in the few weeks she'd been granted, she knew she'd never be able to leave and not look back as she'd originally promised. Ideas on how to extend her stay escaped her, but she was dead certain her life would never be the same again. *She* had a daughter. Regardless of her promise to Sam to the contrary, she wouldn't, couldn't ever forget Melanie Winslow existed, despite the circumstances of her birth.

"All right, where's my daughter?" Sam joked with a smile that didn't quite reach his eyes as he glanced around the young women's department.

"Get over it, Dad," Mel said, and laughed, turning to look at herself in the full-length mirrors. "Rebecca, do you like it?"

"You look beautiful," she whispered, around the sudden lump in her throat. Her child was practically a woman, with gentle curves and a flirtatious smile. That thought brought realization and pain over the lost years. First steps. First words. The discovery of her first butterfly. The wonder of Christmas through a child's eyes or the surprise and delight at discovering the Easter Bunny had indeed hidden a huge basket with a stuffed toy just for her.

She'd missed so much. How could she leave and not be a part of the rest of Melanie's life? She wouldn't be there for first dates or driving lessons. She wouldn't share in the excitement of her daughter's first prom, or the joys and sorrows of first love. Melanie wouldn't come to her for advice on selecting a good college or ask her to accompany her to buy her first car. Well, she'd just have to find a way. It was that simple, and that complicated.

Because this time she would have a choice.

"Rebecca's right," Sam said. "You do look beautiful. And too grown-up," he added with a frown that did nothing to detract from the love and caring in his eyes as he looked at his daughter.

An unexpected rush of tears welled in Rebecca's eyes. She envied her own daughter and the relationship between adoptive father and daughter. A loving relationship filled with mutual respect and caring. Something she'd never had with her own father, even when she'd needed him the most. Something she would never have with her own father.

Mel rolled her eyes and laughed, a sweet, lyrical sound that tugged at Rebecca's already-tender heart. Then she reached up and kissed Sam's cheek. "Dad, you're just gonna have to get over it."

By Friday afternoon Rebecca was convinced she was a fraud. A fake. And a big fat liar. If it didn't come in a box, couldn't be popped into the microwave or picked up at the deli on the corner near her condo, she was lost. As far as cooking went, *hopeless* fit her perfectly.

She wiped her hands on the dish towel tucked into the waistband of her shorts and frowned. She sniffed the air and wrinkled her nose. Carefully, as if afraid something might jump out at her, she lowered the oven door and peered inside. Instead of perfectly round cookies like the picture in the cookbook, the clumps of dough she'd spaced exactly two inches apart as indicated by the directions had run together into a mess of chocolate and dough. The dark brown edges and gooey centers looked hideous, like something out of a cheap horror flick.

She sighed and shrugged. So she'd never be the next Martha Stewart. Law books, not cookbooks, were her forte. She could decipher the most convoluted case law imaginable, but when it came to making something as simple as chocolate chip cookies she was as flat as the thing baking in the oven.

She slipped on the oven mitt and retrieved her disastrous attempt at domesticity from the oven.

"Whatcha bakin', Rebecca?"

Rebecca straightened and headed straight for the garbage can, watching the contents slide off the baking sheet. "It was supposed to be chocolate chip cookies," she told Melanie, then dropped the baking sheet into a pan of soapy water.

"Don't feel bad," Mel said, pulling out a chair to sit at the table. "I can't cook, either. Dad does most of the cooking. He's pretty good, too."

"Your dad's a pretty talented guy," Rebecca said absently, scrubbing baked-on chocolate from the cookie sheet while mentally scratching *cook* off her list of accomplishments.

"Yeah, for a dad and all, he's pretty cool."

The pan would have to soak, she decided. "Let's go for a walk," she suggested. "I need to get out of this room before I scream."

Mel laughed, then stifled a yawn. "You go. I'm a little tired today."

Rebecca tried not to be alarmed, but looked Mel over carefully just the same. Since coming home from the hospital, she had been fairly active, but still tired easily, something the doctors assured them would pass with time.

Rebecca tossed the towel she'd been using as an apron on the counter as Melanie stood and headed toward the door. "Wait a minute," Rebecca called. "What do you mean you can't cook, *either?*"

Mel stopped and gave her an impish grin. She leaned against the doorjamb, crossing her arms over her chest in a remarkable imitation of Sam. "Well, if you *could* cook, why would Wilma Parker bring the meals for you to take out to the hands every day?"

Rebecca planted her hands on her hips and tried to summon an indignant expression. "I have no idea what you're talking about. Wilma and I are friends."

"Uh-huh, sure you are." Melanie laughed, her grin widening. "That's why you give her a check every time she comes to visit. And why she brings tons of food.''

Rebecca bit her lip. Her secret was out. "Does your father know?" she asked, hoping Sam wouldn't call her the fraud she was and order her away from Mel. She needed more time. Who was she trying to kid? She needed a lifetime.

Mel shrugged and looked up at her. "If he does, he isn't saying.''

Rebecca told herself not to worry as she left the house, taking the gravel path toward the barn. The sun was warm and the humidity high, typical, she'd learned, for August in the northern plains. Thick clouds gathered on the horizon, and the first rumble of distant thunder offered the promise of a summer storm. Although the inclement weather made it difficult for the crops to be taken down and carted off to market for sale, she hoped the afternoon thundershower produced enough rain to cool things down.

A shout, followed by the sound of splintering wood, echoed from inside the barn. She didn't hesitate, quickly covering the remaining distance to the barn.

She slipped through the open door and crossed the open area toward the stables and the sound of Sam's deep, smooth voice as he crooned softly from inside one of the stalls. The rich familiar scents of earth and animal, leather and fresh straw swamped her, comforting her.

"Easy now, girl. Easy. Take it easy, sweetheart.''

Her runaway imagination had her fantasizing about Sam speaking to her in the same, soothing, coaxing tones. His hands sliding over her body, exploring, touching, igniting her skin everywhere he touched. Heat pooled in her belly.

"Sam? Are you all right?"

"I'm fine," he said, keeping his attention on the mare. "Stay back. She's a little ticked at me right now."

Rebecca ignored his command and continued to peer over the side of the closed stall. Sam bent low, rubbing a foul-smelling ointment on a nasty-looking cut on the mare's leg.

The mare's eyes rolled back. Her nostrils flared. She kicked the back wall of the stall.

Sam swore.

"Is there anything I can do to help?" Rebecca asked. She might be a disaster zone even standing still in the kitchen, but when it came to horses, Rebecca Martinson was no slouch.

Sam didn't look at her, just continued with his task, dodging when the mare turned to nip at his shoulder with her lethal teeth. "Just stay back," he ordered.

"You really need to calm her down first," she said, reaching over the side to stroke the angry mare's sleek neck. "Doesn't he, baby?"

He applied more salve while Rebecca stroked the mare's neck. Before long, the mare was nudging her hand for more affection and allowing Sam to complete the application process.

"I didn't know you liked horses," he said, wrapping a white bandage around the mare's foreleg. "You've got a touch even this cantankerous old lady responds to."

Rebecca resisted the urge to beam under his praise. "We had horses when I was a kid. I spent a lot of time in the stables." She didn't bother to mention that the stable was the one place she'd never felt like an outsider within her own family.

She reached inside the bucket hanging on a peg outside the stall and scooped a handful of oats, refusing to allow the unpleasant childhood memories to ruin the moment she was sharing with Sam.

He finished with the mare and stepped out of the stall. He looked down at her and frowned. "Thanks," he muttered, then brushed past her.

She let out a sigh. She really shouldn't be surprised by his attitude. Since they'd taken Mel shopping, he'd barely spoken more than two words to her, until today. Still, she tried to be understanding, knowing he considered her a threat to his relationship with Melanie. She had no intention of undermining the closeness he shared with his daughter. She also had no intention of giving up what little she'd gained, either. And if Sam had so much as an inkling of her feelings, he'd run her out of town on a rail—justice Western style.

She moved away from the mare and leaned against a stack of square straw bales against the wall, watching Sam as he forked fresh straw into an empty stall.

She really should get back to the house, but the sight of him held her momentarily spellbound with a longing that shook her to the core.

He wore a blue chambray shirt tucked into a pair of faded jeans that hugged his backside. The scuffed boots added to the same "cowboy" appeal she'd noted when he'd first walked into her office. She watched the corded muscles of arms and back dance beneath the fabric with each swing of the pitchfork and swallowed the wistful sigh hovering on her lips.

He stopped his chore and leaned against the handle of the pitchfork. "Did you want something?" he asked grumpily, the ever-present frown marring his handsome face.

Boy was that ever a loaded question. A slow smile spread across her face. She wanted a lot of things, but right now she wanted Sam Winslow. The realization didn't startle or shame. No matter how ridiculous or foolhardy, she had a serious case of lust close to getting out of control with all the subtlety of a runaway freight train.

He carefully leaned the pitchfork against the wall and slowly walked toward her, intent and purpose evident in his chocolate eyes. She should move. Simply walk out of the barn, but she'd tasted his kisses and heaven help her, she wanted to taste him again. The attraction simmering between them made little sense, but that didn't still the racing of her heart or his steady stride toward her. And she was getting sick and tired of cold showers and restless nights longing for Sam's touch.

"Answer me, Rebecca. What do you want?" His voice was deep and husky, and completely intoxicating. He stopped inches away. All she had to do was reach out, slip her arms around his neck and pull him close to find herself in heaven.

I want you.

The words were so simple, yet more difficult to speak than she'd imagined. Having an affair with Sam would be nothing short of emotional suicide. They had nothing in common, other than their daughter. They lived by different rules; hers dictated by the courtroom, his by the land.

He leaned forward, his eyes darkening, causing the blood to race through her veins. Her pulse quickened and her fingers itched to touch him, to trace the outline of those corded muscles, to run her hands over the hard wall of his chest and feel his heartbeat beneath her palm.

"You," she finally whispered. "I want you."

Sam knew hunger when he saw it, and the hunger in Rebecca's voice mirrored the heat in her eyes. The fire licked at him, teasing him, tempting him, even though he understood the flames would burn him.

Just one taste, he promised himself. Just one brush of her sweet lips. Just one and he'd be satisfied.

He lied.

Heaven help him, regardless of the impending disaster it would surely cause them all, he wanted her with the same kind of hunger that shimmered in her eyes as she looked up at him.

"You don't know what you're asking," he said, bracing his arms on either side of her and leaning close, trapping her between his body and the bales of straw.

"I think I do," she replied, a wicked gleam in her clear green eyes. She slipped her arms around his neck and applied the slightest amount of pressure. It was all the encouragement he needed.

Before she had time to draw her next breath, he pressed his body into hers and captured her lips in a mind-blowing kiss. She responded by pulling him closer. His body hardened instantly. The realization that this was Rebecca, Melanie's birth mother, did nothing to douse the flames leaping to life between them. This woman had the power to destroy his life, yet he couldn't keep his hands off her. Fate had brought them together for its own purposes. Who was he to argue with something he couldn't begin to comprehend?

He skimmed his hand over her hip and down, past those sexy white shorts that showed off her spectacular legs and nearly groaned when he felt her tremble. He cursed the thick denim of his jeans, wanting to feel her skin against his own. He envisioned her silky thighs wrapped around him as they surrendered to the ancient rhythm of man and woman. He wanted to taste every inch of her sweet body and lose himself in her heat. The fact that she wanted the same thing was more powerful than any aphrodisiac known to man.

He slipped his hands down to her bottom, urging them closer together. She whimpered and moved her hips against him, causing him to nearly come out of his skin. What little control he had left was rapidly deteriorating. He no longer doubted they'd make love, but not here, not in the barn where anyone could walk in and discover them, especially Mel.

Regardless of the pain it cost him, he settled his hands on her hips and gently eased her away from him. When she looked up at him, her eyes filled with longing and desire, his good intentions evaporated.

He kissed her again. Slow and deep. Long and wet.

He heard the shouts of the men coming in from the fields, not sure whether to curse their timing or be grateful. He was behaving like a testosterone-overloaded teenager, willing to carry her off to the loft and make love. But when he made love to Rebecca, it wouldn't be a quick roll in the hay. Oh, no, when they made love, he wanted it to be long and slow, hard and fast, and totally consuming.

He pulled away, shocked by the overwhelming disappointment he felt at the loss of heat.

"Later," he promised, kissing her one last time. "Later, when we won't be interrupted."

Rebecca nodded, unable to move as Sam strode out of the barn as if he hadn't just promised to turn her world upside down. Good God, what was she doing? If she'd had the energy, she would have laughed. She knew exactly what she was doing—making a mistake of epic proportions.

A monumental mistake, but one she would never regret. Whether it made sense or not, she was falling hard for her daughter's father.

Chapter Eight

Rebecca set the porch swing in motion with the toe of her sneaker. The balmy evening, combined with the sound of rain pattering softly against the roof should have calmed her.

It didn't.

Later.

The word had the ability to make her insides flutter and her heart race.

Later.

She closed her eyes and rested her head against the back of the swing. Erotic images filtered through her mind. Tangled sheets. Tangled bodies. Tangled hearts.

Later.

Sam's dark eyes filling with heat and passion as he brought them together in a maelstrom of electricity and heat.

Later. Later. Later!

She snapped her eyes open.

Restless energy, *not* sexual frustration, she told herself firmly, made her skin feel tight and her insides like melted butter. She left the swing and crossed the wide veranda to the railing, where she braced her hands on the smooth wooden surface. She leaned forward to gaze out over the expanse of front lawn, mentally listing 101 reasons why making love to Sam Winslow would be wrong.

For every reason not to, her rebuttal was constant: she wanted him. *Badly.*

The realization alone should have had her packing her bags and hitchhiking, if necessary, to Minot to catch the first flight back to Los Angeles. But *frigid* was never a word she could attribute to herself, regardless of the nightmares of her past. Her marriage hadn't failed because she was sexually unresponsive but because they'd never really been in love in the first place.

The squeak of the screen door snagged her attention. She looked over her shoulder and her heart rate accelerated. *Was it,* she thought, pulling in a shaky breath, *later?*

Sam moved silently toward her, then turned and propped his backside against the railing. He'd showered. His hair was damp, and he smelled of soap. He didn't say anything, but she saw the flare of a match as he lit his nightly cigarette, followed by a plume of blue smoke.

Nervous, and at a total loss for words, she straightened and leaned her shoulder against the post. She slipped her trembling hands inside the pockets of her shorts and sucked in a deep breath, letting it out slowly.

Think about your cases. Think about poor Peter Grant and how he could lose his parental rights. The case was special to her, but no one at Denison, Ross & Furnari would ever know the deep empathy she kept buried inside for Peter Grant and other clients like him. Signed documents existed, stating she'd legally relinquished all rights to her child, but if she truly wanted to fight to regain those rights, she could. Her chances of winning would be slim at best, based on the length of time Melanie had lived with Sam, but she was a good lawyer and knew she could convince the courts she deserved visitation. She would even settle for supervised visitation.

Except she would never do it. Melanie belonged with Sam. *He* was her father. And she would never do anything to hurt her daughter.

As much as she hated to admit it, her own father was right about one thing, she *was* being selfish. Important careers could be destroyed if she wasn't careful. She wasn't quite so melodramatic to believe that the fate of the nation was at stake, even if her father probably believed that to be the case.

"You looking awfully serious tonight," Sam said, his voice a sensual rumble that skirted along her nerve endings. "What are you thinking about?"

"A trial that's coming up when I get back home." She despised the reference to the end of her time in North Dakota. *Home* meant Los Angeles, and miles away from the two people who were becoming more important to her every day.

Her daughter.

And Sam.

He took a deep drag on the cigarette. "You enjoy practicing law, don't you?" he asked after a moment.

"I do," she said, forcing herself to relax. "Especially family law. But there are perks and disappointments, just like any other career."

She pushed away from the post and edged closer to him, resting her bottom against the railing and bracing her hands behind her. "What about you?" she asked him, willing her pulse rate to slow. "Is farming the be all end all, for you, Winslow?"

He took another drag of the cigarette, then looked at her with narrowed eyes. "It's a living."

His brusque tone surprised her. Though their choice in professions were miles apart in nature, they were no less successful. She surveyed the surrounding area, the manicured lawn, several barns and outbuildings in the distance and rich farmland as far as the eye could see. "Looks like a pretty good living to me. Aren't you happy?"

He shrugged. "Why shouldn't I be?" he answered cryptically, then stubbed out his cigarette. "What about you, Counselor?" He shifted and stood above her. His deep-brown eyes held an intensity that had nothing to do with heated passion or *later,* but she couldn't define the source. "Are you happy?"

"I used to think so," she stated honestly. She'd

accomplished plenty in her life, but her accomplishments were career oriented and marred by a past she
would never be able to completely forget, nor did she
want to. Her past made her what she was today. She
had a failed marriage and could count her close
friends on one hand. The long hours she spent at the
firm made socializing outside of the office difficult,
not to mention dates with the opposite sex. A long
time ago she'd faced the fact that men willing to com-
pete with her long hours were practically nonexistent.

Professionally she had no complaints. Personally
she was no longer certain.

He crossed his arms over his wide chest and braced
his feet apart. "But now you don't know?"

She straightened, recognizing the intensity in his
eyes as anger. Why, or from where it stemmed, she
wasn't certain, but quickly decided treading lightly
would be a wise choice until she could determine the
source.

"I'm successful and that makes me happy. And it
might sound egotistical, but I'm only thirty-one years
old and already a junior partner. You don't achieve
that kind of success without making a few sacrifices
along the way."

"What was your great sacrifice?" he asked in a
low, determined voice. "Giving away a kid to save
the great Martinsons from the shame of having a bastard in the family? Very noble, Rebecca."

She didn't think, but reacted instead—with the
stinging slap of her palm connecting with Sam's

cheek. His eyes glittered dangerously, sending a slight shiver of fear sliding down her spine.

"I'm sorry," she murmured, too shaken by her violent outburst to offer more than a simple apology. Before she could make an even bigger fool of herself or tell him that he was absolutely right, she stepped around him and headed down the steps, breathing a sigh of relief when he made no attempt to stop her. The confusion of the present was melding with that of the past, and she needed time alone, time to sort out the mess she was making of things.

Using the light of the full moon peeking through the patchy storm clouds as her guide, she followed the gravel path to the stables and slipped through the side door. Incandescent lights hung in intervals from the rafters along the row of stalls, bathing the area in a soft, buttery glow. She moved down the row of stalls until she came to the mare Sam had doctored earlier.

The horse nickered softly in greeting, stretching her sleek neck over the half door in search of attention. Rebecca rubbed the mare's velvety muzzle, then reached inside the bucket for a handful of oats. "You sure know a sucker when you see one, don't you, old girl?"

The mare tossed her head, as if nodding in agreement, making Rebecca smile despite the churning in her stomach. She couldn't remember when she'd ever reacted so violently, and she was appalled by her be-

havior. Hadn't she'd been taught from an early age
the potency of verbal weapons?

This isn't the time for noble actions, Rebecca.

She tried to block out the painful memories, but the
hurtful words she'd kept buried for too many years
rushed forward. What was so noble in having your
child taken away from you? The only noble thing
she'd ever done was never attempt to find her baby,
because by then, it had been too late. She would never
hurt her unknown child by tearing her world apart.

*I will not allow you to sacrifice the good name of
this family.*

She continued to stroke the mare, desperately seeking comfort. Except this time the familiar scents and
sounds of her childhood sanctuary failed to soothe
her.

A bastard!

"Don't call her that," she whispered, fighting to
hold back a rush of tears. "My baby is not a bastard.
Not anymore."

She let out a long, shuddering breath and refused
to cry. Instead she concentrated on the scents and
sounds surrounding her: the rustle of horses, the sweet
smell of fresh straw mingled with oiled leather and
tack. As a child she'd often escaped to the stables.
There, no one had cared she was outspoken or had a
mind of her own. No one had sighed in exasperation
whenever she was around. There, she'd found solace
from the loneliness of her own home.

More bitter memories assailed her, taking her back

to the time she'd hidden in the hayloft and had fallen asleep, crying from the deep hurt caused by her father's angry words. She'd awoken long after dark, fearful of another tirade, certain her family would have been frantically searching for her.

She bit back a sob at the ache the memory still caused. She'd returned to the house hours later, the moon riding high in the night sky, and had slipped inside through the kitchen, prepared to meet and receive her punishment for frightening her family with her lengthy disappearance.

Only no one had been waiting for her. No one had missed the nine-year-old daughter of the manor.

Sam silently closed the door behind him and stood watching Rebecca. She rested her forehead against the rough wooden post, her shoulders slumped forward in a show of defeat. She murmured something unintelligible to the horse and turned, stopping when she spotted him.

He pushed away from the door and moved slowly toward her. "I deserved that," he said, giving her a half smile and rubbing at the still-stinging spot on his cheek. He hadn't meant to be such a jerk, but her questions about happiness had frightened him, making him wonder, and worry, if she would attempt to fight him for Mel. "I'm the one who owes you an apology."

She pulled in a deep breath, the movement emphasizing the fullness of her breasts. God help him, he wanted this woman. Making love to Rebecca would be a major complication in an already complicated existence, but the knowledge failed to suppress the constant need that nearly exploded with life whenever he came within ten feet of her, or the restless nights he'd spent tossing and turning just thinking of her sleek body beneath his. They were headed for disaster. A disaster he was helpless to prevent.

"You're not being fair," she said, her voice so soft he had to strain to hear her. "You have no idea what it was like for me back then."

"Then enlighten me."

She had secrets. If she'd be honest with him, tell him about her past, maybe they could stop circling each other like two wary dogs.

She turned, but not before he saw the emotions in her gaze: pain and fear. The pain, he thought he understood. The fear confused him and heightened his curiosity. What could she possibly fear?

She stepped up to the straw bales and sat on the lowest stack, scooting until her back rested against the wall. Pulling her long legs to her chest, she rested her chin on her updrawn knees and wrapped her slender arms around her legs. The moments ticked by, and he didn't think she was going to tell him. He sighed and strode down the center of the stables toward her.

"Rebecca," he called softly. She looked at him, but the expression in her eyes was faraway, as if she'd already begun recalling the events surrounding the de-

cision to give her child up for adoption. A decision
that she'd claimed again and again hadn't been hers.

He sat beside her and reached for her hand, closing
his fingers around her more slender ones. "You want
me to be fair, Rebecca, then you have to tell me. What
happened? You said you didn't have a choice. Everyone has choices, but sometimes we just make the
wrong one."

She shook her head, but wouldn't look at him. "It
wasn't like that. The decision *wasn't* mine," she said,
her voice wavering with the tears he didn't think
she'd ever shed.

Damn her, he thought. Why was it so important for
her to be so tough? He wasn't a fool. He'd watched
her, more than he should, for the past two weeks.
Anyone could see she was really a marshmallow inside. She was a caring and gentle woman with an
energy that amazed him. He admired her willingness
to help without question, even when he knew she was
completely out of her element. Her passion for life in
general matched his own, as did her determination
and drive to succeed. They had more in common than
he'd initially realized; a commonality stretched between them beyond the invisible bond they shared
with Mel. Certainly, they came from different worlds,
and he knew from experience that a lasting relationship between them would never work. But he was
drawn to her, and as hard as he'd tried to keep his
distance, he was failing miserably.

He gave her fingers entwined with his a gentle

squeeze. "Talk to me," he urged with equal gentleness.

"It was my seventeenth birthday and everything was so magical," she started, her voice filled with the same faraway quality as her eyes. "My father never did anything half measure, and when his only daughter turned seventeen and was accepted to his alma mater in the same week, it was an excuse to pull out all the stops and throw the party of the season." She laughed, a caustic sound with no humor. "I had really wanted to go to Brown. They'd accepted me, too, but for the first time in my life, *I'd* done something that made my father proud of me. I tore up the acceptance letter and never told him."

He understood family pressure all too well. He'd been forced to give up his own career choice to return home to the family business when his father's health deteriorated.

"And it was some party," she said, turning to face him, resting her cheek against her knees. "Twinkling white lights in the trees, along the path to the stables and throughout the gardens. A huge tent set up over the tennis court for dining and dancing. A buffet catered by Sacramento's best five-star restaurant and champagne chilled to perfection. Music. Laughter. I felt very grown-up. Too grown-up."

She pulled her hand from his grasp, scooted off the bales and started to pace. He remained silent, waiting for her to continue. Her brows were pulled into a frown when she stopped to look at him.

"Craig was there," she finally said. She rubbed at her temple, then shoved her hands in the pockets of her shorts, but not before he noticed they were trembling. "He's Melanie's biological father," she added in a rush, then let out a breath and began pacing again.

Sam couldn't be certain, but he suspected there was more, much more about the identity of Mel's parentage than she was willing to tell him. For now he let it drop.

"Our parents had been friends for years—they ran in the same circle. The country club set," she said in a haughty tone, waving her hand in the air as she paced. "Anyway, Craig was a couple years older than me and already a sophomore at Brown. I'd had a crush on him for as long as I could remember.

"For my birthday my father bought me a horse, a beautiful Thoroughbred that I was so proud of, and I'd convinced Craig to sneak down to the stables with me so I could show off my present. I stole a bottle of champagne and two glasses from the bar when the bartender wasn't looking. Craig and I never made it to the stables. We slipped into the gazebo in the rose garden. He kissed me, a birthday kiss, he'd said."

She let out a slow, even breath before pulling another deeply into her lungs.

Fear, anticipation and an unexplainable fury bubbled up inside him as he waited for her to continue.

A wry grin tugged at the corners of her mouth. "I'd had too much champagne, and in all honesty I probably let things go too far before I said no. My biggest mistake that night was in believing Craig returned my feelings. I realized later how wrong I was."

She stopped pacing and came to stand in front of him. He thought of Mel, and how she meant everything to him. How could he continue to condemn Rebecca when the circumstances of Mel's conception were not her fault?

"Rebecca, no means no. Don't make excuses for him."

She sat beside him on the bale, her sweet scent wrapping around him, distracting him. If he'd been the one in the rose garden, could he have kept his hands off her? If she'd said no, damn straight he would have.

"Would you believe he never called me again?" she said, plucking a piece of straw and twisting it between her fingers. "He never knew I was going to have his baby. I did see him again, two weeks after that night in the gardens, but he blamed me. Called me a tease and a few other unflattering names. I was crushed."

"So you decided to give your child away?"

She shook her head and looked at him. "No," she stated emphatically. "Two months later when I found out I was pregnant, I had every intention of keeping my child. Abortion wasn't an option for me, and I never once considered adoption. I knew raising a child wouldn't be easy, especially considering the circumstances, but this was *my* baby and I was more than willing to make whatever sacrifices were necessary. It didn't take a rocket scientist to know that once my father found out he would be furious with me. He blamed me, Sam. I almost expected that from him, but I never dreamed he'd give my child away.''

Sam's heart twisted for the young, confused girl she'd been, faced with adult decisions long before she'd been emotionally equipped to deal with them. ''You keep saying you didn't have a choice about keeping Mel. How could you not have had a choice?''

The smile she gave him was self-deprecating at best. ''You don't know my father,'' she said, her tone wry. ''I was seventeen and still in high school. I'd fought like hell to make him understand that I didn't want to give up my child. But when it came right down to it, I *didn't* have a choice. I was still a minor, Sam. As my legal guardian, my father signed the adoption papers.''

He stared at her, disbelief etched on his handsome features. And then he exploded, uttering a string of vile curses. He rose and stalked across the area, turned and looked at her—anger, pain and fear adding to the emotions swirling in his dark eyes.

''Are you telling me that Mel is not legally my daughter? *You* never signed away *your* parental rights?'' he thundered.

Rebecca shook her head, thinking furiously. There was so much more to tell him, so many more secrets that he could never know, and yet, she'd revealed far too much already. She'd told him what she'd never told another living soul besides her parents.

And they hadn't believed her.

She sucked in a deep breath and let it out slow. She left her perch and stepped in front of him, placing her hand on his chest. His heart beat heavily against her palm.

"No, Sam. Melanie is *your* daughter. Right here," she said, gently tapping his chest, "right here where it counts more than anything."

He braced his hands on his hips and looked to the rafters. After a moment he shook his head and gazed down at her again. "I can't believe this. Your father signed away *your* rights."

Slowly she lowered her hand to her side. "You have to know I would *never* attempt to take Melanie away from you."

His eyebrows clashed over his dark-brown eyes. "How can I be sure? A technicality exists. Doesn't that void my daughter's adoption?"

"Legally it could, but I wouldn't ever, *ever* do that. I won't hurt Melanie." She offered him a weak grin. "Or you," she added on a softer note.

He stepped away from her and faced the stalls, rubbing at the back of his neck. He muttered another curse and shook his head again. "Was your father already on the Supreme Court?" he asked, keeping his back to her.

No matter how angry she was with her father, she did love him, and the last thing she wanted was to destroy his career. But Sam deserved to know the truth. "Yes."

"Could he lose his appointment over this?"

"I'm not sure. Certain case laws prohibit minors from signing away their parental rights. Legally I was underage and unable to enter a binding contract, but as my guardian he could on my behalf. It's a sticky legal situation."

He spun around to face her, anger blazing in his eyes. "You're a lawyer," he snapped. "Can I lose Mel?"

"I told you. I have no intention of attempting to take Melanie away from you. *You* are her father. I'm only her birth mother."

"But you didn't have a choice, remember? It wasn't right, Rebecca." He took a deep breath in what she thought was an effort to calm himself. She knew he wasn't angry with her, but at the situation, and he had every right. If he knew who Mel's biological father really was, he would probably explode.

She crossed the small space separating them and slipped her arms around his middle. He looked down at her, the anger fading slightly from his gaze.

"Sam, when I first came here, I admit it, I was curious. I'd wondered if I'd done the right thing in not fighting for my legal rights as Melanie's mother. I think I wanted assurance that I'd done the right thing. But I learned something else. Something that's much more important than either one of our perceived rights. Melanie has something I never had. Something special. She shares a relationship with her father built on trust and mutual respect. Isn't that what really matters?''

He let out a ragged breath and pulled her close. They stood together, the sounds of the horses and the rhythmic patter of rain on the roof surrounding them. The familiar scents that had once provided her comfort as a child offered the same now, but she found something more in Sam's arms, and it frightened and exhilarated her at the same time. She knew she could fall for Sam, she just hadn't expected it to happen.

He stroked her back, moving upward with his hand to cup the back of her neck, applying enough pressure for her to look up at him. ''I love my daughter,'' he said, his eyes filled with emotion. ''I would *never* treat her like your father has you.''

''I know you wouldn't,'' she whispered.

''What about this Craig? Couldn't he try to come after Mel?''

She shook her head. ''You don't have to worry about Craig,'' she said. At least that much was the truth. Except Craig wasn't the threat. ''He died about ten years ago in a car accident.''

He let out a ragged sigh filled with relief. ''So where do we go from here?'' he asked, continuing to stroke her back.

Heat pooled in her belly, and her body yearned for his touch. ''I have an idea,'' she teased, in an attempt at levity, and gave him her most wicked grin. He chuckled in response.

There'd been too many revelations, too many truths spoken tonight that would forever change the course of their relationship. For the first time since Sam had walked into her office, she felt a sense of hope for the future—a future that included her being a part of her daughter's life. How, she wasn't certain, but at least she had hope. And she wouldn't ask for more.

Chapter Nine

"I can't believe I let you talk me into this," Sam complained to his daughter. "A dance of all things."

He rinsed the razor under the steaming tap water and looked at Mel through the mirror. She sat on the edge of the tub watching him shave, rolling eyes that sparkled with mischief. "You'll have fun, Dad. If you stop complaining."

He grunted in reply before turning his head to the side to slide the razor over the stubble on his cheek. He didn't doubt he'd have a good time with Rebecca, only he had something much more intimate in mind. Like the kind of dancing better served between the sheets than on a dance floor.

"What time is Leah's mom picking you up?" he asked, tapping the razor on the edge of the sink. Mel insisted she didn't need a baby-sitter, and he agreed, but that didn't mean he was willing to leave his daughter alone so soon after being released from the hospital. Her strength was coming back, and she was quickly returning to her old self, but he still worried.

The only reason he'd capitulated to her arm twisting was under the proviso she not be left alone. A quick phone call to her best friend, Leah, had solved that problem. And now he was taking Rebecca to the annual Harvest dance, forced to be in a roomful of a hundred or so townsfolk while holding a beautiful woman in his arms on a sawdust-covered dance floor, when he really wanted to be alone with her.

He still hadn't come to terms with the bombshell she'd dropped in his lap last night. The thought that his adoption of Mel could be invalid scared the hell out of him. Mel was *his* daughter. Hell, she was his life, and the thought of losing her was too dreadful a scenario to even contemplate. He had a solution in mind, but he hadn't yet broached the subject with Rebecca. There was a chance she could stonewall him, and then where would he be?

He rinsed the remaining traces of shaving cream from his face, then buried his face in a rich, burgundy towel. No matter how much he wanted Rebecca, one thing was perfectly clear: he'd fight her with everything he had to keep his daughter.

The storm that had been brewing for most of the day had finally arrived, signaled by a loud crack of thunder followed by a flickering of the lights. Judging by the sound of Mother Nature's tempest, they'd be lucky if they even made it to the Harvest Dance.

"Are you going to wear *that* shirt?" Mel asked with a wrinkling of her pert nose when she followed him into the bedroom.

He picked up the red-plaid cotton shirt he'd set out before his shower. "What's wrong with my shirt?"

Mel rolled her eyes. "Dad, you want to look nice, don't you?" She crossed the room to the closet and peered inside. "Here." She retrieved a hunter-green dress shirt and handed it to him. "And this," she added, slipping a tie in maroon, chocolate and gold paisley from the rack.

"I'm not wearing a tie to a dance," he protested, crossing his arms over his chest. "So you can just forget it."

Mel sighed. "Dad, you're taking a woman out for a night on the town. You can't wear *that!*" She pointed to the shirt in his hands as if he was considering a public display of long johns and greasy overalls.

Mel flung the tie over her shoulder and snagged the offensive shirt from his hand. "You have to wear a tie. Women like men in ties."

"It's a barn dance, for crying out loud," he complained, slipping his arms into the shirt she'd chosen. "And what do you know about men who wear ties."

"I've read *Cosmo*." She had the audacity to giggle at his frown. "And ditch the T-shirt. Men who don't wear T-shirts under their dress shirts are sexier. That way, when she unbuttons—"

He gaped at his daughter. "You're not to read *Cosmo* again, young lady. Do you hear me?"

Mel sighed and ignored him. She planted her hands on her hips and frowned again. "Dad?"

"What now?"

"The boots. They have to go."

He dropped on the edge of the bed and pulled on a pair of thick socks. "I've been dressing myself for a long time, Mel." He could live with the dress shirt and even the tie, albeit reluctantly, but he was wearing a T-shirt *and* his boots. A man had to draw the line somewhere.

Mel plopped next to him. "Sheesh, Dad. Get with the program. You want to impress her, right?"

He reached for his boots and stopped. "Impress who?" he asked, straightening.

Mel slipped her arm through his and giggled. "Very funny. Rebecca, that's who. Face it, Dad. You've got the hots for her. I can tell."

He frowned, and felt more than slightly disgruntled that his fourteen-year-old daughter could tell when her dad had the "hots" for a woman. "We're friends," he answered, reaching for his boots.

"More than friends," she corrected, giving his arm a squeeze before letting go. "You are *so* obvious. You're not nervous, are you?"

"I am not nervous." He shoved his foot into the boot, then tugged his jeans over the top. "You have an overactive imagination."

"Anyone can see the way you guys have been looking at each another all week."

He slipped on the other boot. "And how is that?" he asked, hoping he sounded more nonchalant than he felt. There was something wrong in the world when he was being interrogated by his own kid, not to mention listening to her advice on how to attract the opposite sex.

He sat up straight and looked at her, waiting for her to answer. Faded jeans, ripped at the knee, covered her long coltish legs. She'd be tall, probably as tall as her birth mother in another year or two, and once she passed through the awkwardness of youth, she'd more than likely move with the same sleek grace as Rebecca. Despite the ratty jeans and one of his T-shirts she was in the habit of helping herself to lately, his daughter was a beautiful girl. She was growing up way too fast to suit him, and he'd give just about anything to be able to turn back the clock and extend their time together. He could very well find himself a grandfather in another ten years. And that made him feel very old.

"Well?" he prodded.

Mel gave him an impish grin and laughed, a sound that made his heart warm, despite the outrageousness of their conversation. "I dunno. All goofy-eyed, I guess."

"Goofy-eyed?"

"Uh-huh." She laughed again and handed him the tie she'd chosen. "Like you want to kiss her all the time."

"Where do you get this stuff?" he complained, embarrassed that even his daughter could see his attraction to Rebecca. He crossed the room to the bureau, slipped the tie around his neck and worked the knot.

Mel sighed and scooted onto the center of his king-size bed, crossing her long legs Indian-style. "I'm not a child."

"Hey, you're still my little girl." He stifled a curse when the tie had to be redone. Why had he let her talk him into this? First the dance, and now a blasted tie.

"Dad, get over it, would ya? Even I have to grow up sometime."

"Fine, can you just do it a little slower, please?"

By his third attempt with the tie, he was ready to chuck the whole thing. Maybe Mel was right. Maybe he was nervous. He peered at his reflection. He was definitely not "goofy-eyed."

Mel left the bed and moved to stand in front of him. "Let me." She worked the knot, getting it right the first time. "Almost perfect," she declared, then moved to the closet, returning with a dark-brown corduroy jacket.

He tucked in his shirt, then took the jacket without argument. Like it would do any good, he thought, to argue with a determined fourteen-year-old female.

"Now remember to compliment her," Mel said, giving him a final once-over. "Tell her how great she looks." She made a minor adjustment to his tie.

Satisfied, she handed him his wallet. "And remember to open her door for her, hold her chair, gentleman stuff. Girls really like that."

She scooped his change off the dresser and waited while he stuffed his wallet in his back pocket before handing him the coins. "And get her plate for her."

He pocketed the change and picked up his keys. "Should I cut her meat for her, too?" he grumbled.

She swiped at his shoulder and plucked a piece of lint from the jacket. "Dad, be serious," she said with a frown.

He raised his hands in defeat and chuckled. "Enough, Mel. I've done this sort of thing before, okay?"

She smiled, looped her arms around his neck and planted a kiss on his cheek. "It's been a while. You might be, you know, kinda rusty."

He slipped his arm around her shoulders and steered her toward the door. "Whether or not I'm rusty is my business, okay?"

"I'm just trying to help," she said, her melodramatic tone causing him to chuckle. "I don't want people saying my dad doesn't know how to show a woman a good time."

Oh, yeah. He was right. There was no arguing with a determined female—no matter what her age.

By the time they reached the foot of the stairs, Rebecca was waiting for him. His mouth went dry, and a surge of heat headed south when he took in the woman standing with her back to the fireplace. Lightning flashed, followed by a deep roll of thunder, matching the turmoil inside him.

She wore black—a short, linen-type dress with cap

sleeves, a square neck and a hemline that showed off miles of leg. The only break in color came from the emerald earrings at her lobes that matched the rich emerald of her eyes. And her lips: full, luscious and red, like ripe, sweet cherries. He couldn't take his eyes off those lips, and his imagination ran wild.

The sound of a honking horn broke the spell, but not before he saw the look in Rebecca's eyes. A look filled with heat, desire and longing. If this was what Mel meant by goofy-eyed, then he wasn't complaining. "You're absolutely beautiful," he said.

She blushed, a slight heightening of color to her cheeks that made her look even more desirable. "Thank you."

"Well, hey, that's Leah's mom," Mel said, grinning widely. She stuffed her hands in the back pockets of her jeans. "I'll be running along now. You kids have fun."

His good sense returned, and he stopped Mel before she could bolt out the door. "I'll be right back," he told Rebecca, then picked up Mel's overnight bag and followed her outside.

The winds had gained momentum, but the rain had yet to fall. It was only a matter of time, judging by the ferocity of the storm brewing. He spoke to Leah's mom, kissed Mel goodbye and made her promise not to stay up all night. As he stood on the porch watching the red taillights disappear down the country road, he realized that he and Rebecca would be alone tonight.

All night, he thought, before going back inside to the woman who had the power to make him lose total and complete control.

He could hardly wait.

THE VARIETY OF NIGHT SPOTS and dance clubs in Los Angeles couldn't come close to capturing the authenticity and down-home feel of a true midwestern barn dance. Paper streamers replaced neon lights. A potluck buffet substituted for elegant, five-star cuisine. Folding chairs and paper plates were exchanged for fine linen and china. Long-necked beer kept on ice in galvanized steel tubs or boxed wine in plastic cups were served in place of Long Island iced teas or Mexican mud slides.

Rebecca couldn't remember the last time she'd had so much fun.

The raging thunderstorm failed to put a damper on the partygoers as raucous laughter rose above the din of country-western music and voices engaged in conversation. She tapped her foot to the snappy country song the DJ played, listening to Linda Crawford explain the how-tos of quilting. The closest Rebecca had ever come to a sewing machine was the fitting room at her tailor's on Rodeo Drive, but she felt completely at ease, even as the conversation shifted to the more foreign topics of vegetable gardens and canning, crafts and baked goods, 4H and FFA.

Husbands sat with their wives, arguing with the other men at their table on the varying causes of low grain yields and the rising costs of farming. Although Sam was embroiled in the discussion, he still managed to make her feel weak with longing. She strongly suspected his hand resting on her knee and his fingers absently tracing little circles on the inside of her thigh as a contributing factor to her state of continual arousal.

The snappy little tune segued into another, and the women pushed away from the table. "Come on, Rebecca," Barbara Longwood called. "Time for you to learn another line dance."

"Let go of her, Sam," Wilma Parker teased, when he grabbed her hand, preventing her from leaving. "We'll bring her back soon."

The men laughed, and Rebecca set her beer on the table. She stood, her hand still clasped with Sam's. When he looked up at her with desire-filled eyes, her insides fluttered.

"Save it for the bedroom, Sammy. This is a public place," Nancy Hooper added to the jests, causing further laughter.

Rebecca blushed but couldn't help the happiness bubbling to the surface. Were they that obvious?

Sam let her go, and his reluctance made her heart soar. Tonight their differences had been left behind. Tonight no one questioned if their being together was right or if they were making an enormous error in judgment. Tonight Sam wanted her. Tonight there was no question about *later*. They would make love, and she held no illusions to the contrary.

She stepped onto the dance floor with the other women from their table. Paying attention to the steps they showed her became difficult because she couldn't keep her gaze from straying to Sam. He'd pushed his chair away from the table and blatantly watched her. His unguarded attention should have made her awkward and clumsy, instead she felt sexy and just a little wanton.

Linda and Wilma flanked her, and she followed their examples, but when the line dance called for her to circle her hips, she did so with deliberate slowness, and never took her eyes off Sam. She hid a smile when he loosened his tie as if he suddenly found breathing difficult.

She continued, using the steps and the music as a masked sort of foreplay, careful not to be too risqué, considering they were in public. The overtures weren't missed by Sam, and she was rewarded by heat flaring in his eyes and the way he continually shifted in his chair. She could hear the good-natured ribbing coming from the other men at their table, but Sam took the slaps on the back and ribald jests in stride.

The dance called for a skip-like movement and she did so, inching her dress slightly higher and giving him a sultry smile. Sam lifted a brow as he watched her, then tugged on his tie again.

Before the song ended he was by her side, sliding his arms around her and whisking her away in a two-step. She heard Linda comment about somebody getting lucky, followed by more laughter, but she didn't care. To hell with repercussions, she thought. She wanted Sam more than she'd ever wanted any other man, and there would be no stopping them from making love tonight.

The music changed to something slower and more romantic, and he brought their bodies in closer contact. When he slid his hand up her back to cup her neck and rested his cheek against her temple, a fluttering sensation started in her tummy.

"You don't play fair, Counselor," he said, his voice strained and tight.

She smiled and reached up to nip at his ear with her teeth. "It's called foreplay, honey. And there's plenty more where that came from."

His fingers on the back of her neck flexed and she sensed his slipping control. If she wasn't careful, they could end up making love in the back seat of his car like a couple of hormonal teenagers.

"Do you know what you're doing to me?" he growled.

She moved with the music and brushed her breasts across his wide chest. He groaned in response, then held her tight against him as he spun her around the dance floor. The song ended, and she reluctantly slipped out of his embrace. Reaching upward, she planted a kiss on his lips and smiled. "What's the matter, plowboy?" she teased in a deliberately sultry tone. "Things getting a little too hot for you?"

She turned to head back to their table, but he placed

both hands on her shoulders and held her still. Her breath halted when he leaned forward. His warm breath caressed the back of her neck, causing a shiver to race down her spine.

"Babe, you haven't seen hot." His tongue traced a quick path from her ear to the base of her neck. "Yet," he added with erotic promise.

The fluttering butterflies in her tummy converted into a flock of birds and took flight. Sweet anticipation hummed through her veins. She couldn't wait to get home.

He stepped around her and chuckled, leaving her standing alone on the dance floor. It took her a moment to recover, but she eventually followed him to their table. By the time she reached his side, he was already saying his goodbyes. She thanked the women for teaching her how to line dance, but was careful not to make any promises of future social gatherings when they asked if she'd be staying in Shelbourne.

"Ready?" Sam asked.

The look in his eyes held her spellbound. Oh, yes, she was ready. More than ready. She nodded, because she didn't trust her voice.

He took hold of her hand and steered her around the perimeter of the dance floor to the exit. The earlier rainstorm had abated temporarily, but occasional lightning flashed across the sky, followed by the answer of distant thunder. After the warmth from inside the barn, she shivered when the night air brushed against her skin.

"Come here," Sam said, his voice a husky, sensual rumble that made her heart rate triple. He slipped his jacket over her shoulders and used the lapels to pull her close. His arms circled her and held her tight.

She tipped her head back, waiting for him to kiss her. He did. There was nothing gentle about the kiss. This was a kiss by a man with clear intent—to possess the woman in his arms in the most elemental way possible between a man and a woman. She sagged against him, craving the feel of his hard and lean body against hers.

As his tongue swept across hers in the sweet rhythmic motion as ancient as time itself, she searched her mind for any lasting reservations concerning the final line that she and Sam were crossing. Only one remained, and that was that she hadn't been completely honest with him about Melanie's background. For a brief instant she considered telling him, but the thought fled just as quickly. That was one detail she would always keep to herself, because despite her father's accusations of selfishness, she would not do anything that could destroy the lives of so many people, especially Sam and Melanie.

Confident she was making the right decision, she splayed her hands over Sam's chest. He groaned, a deep rough sound that made her wish for privacy. Voices rose, and music floated out of the barn, but the world around her slowly receded until there was only the two of them and the desire and need driving them both closer to the edge where control ceased and only sensation existed.

The sound of laughter drifted to her through the sensual fog in her mind. Sam lifted his head. "Not here," he said, and moved them away from the path in the makeshift parking lot to the shadows at the side of the barn.

She should have protested. She should have stopped him, but the need crashing through her overrode common sense. "I want you. Now, Sam."

"Easy, babe," he whispered, while his hot, damp mouth trailed kisses along her throat.

His fingers brushed her thigh and slipped beneath the hem of her dress. She whimpered, no longer shocked by the force of her desire for Sam. Her body sought his, creating its own siren call with dampening need.

He inched her dress up, exposing the tops of her lacy stockings. The warm, sultry air brushed against her skin, adding to the heat rather than cooling. He kissed her deeply while his fingers traced the outline of her stockings, moving slowly upward to where she craved his touch.

He used his body to shield her, and she felt perfectly safe regardless of the risks of exposure. She was past caring; she wanted Sam, needed him. He brushed his fingers against her moist curls and stilled. He lifted his head and stared at her, disbelief evident in her gaze. "You're not wearing…"

She smiled lazily. "Nope."

His breathing increased and he rested his forehead against hers. "Sweet heaven, Rebecca," he whispered. He didn't sound ashamed or appalled, just very turned on, as she'd intended. "Woman, you'll be the death of me, I swear it."

"Sam?"

"Hmm?"

"Shut up and finish what you started."

He chuckled, a deep, rough sound that bordered on a growl. "Whatever you want, babe," he said against her lips, before pulling her into a storm of sensation. He kissed her long and deep, slow and wet, making love to her mouth until she lost track of everything around her but Sam and the fire racing through her veins. One hand cupped her bare bottom while he sought her slick heat with the other.

He stroked, as if familiar with the secrets of her body, instinctively knowing just how to make her come apart in his arms. Her body tensed, closing around his fingers as she edged closer to the climax he kept just out of her reach. She bowed against him, and he caught her before she slipped over the edge, his mouth capturing her cries of release as she rode the crest of her completion.

She clung to him, breathing hard, certain her heart and body would never be the same again. Tenderly he straightened her clothes, then held her against him while her senses returned to normal. His own breathing was unsteady as he stroked her back and kissed the dampness at her temple. She was amazed at his restraint in denying his own need, which only served to heighten her anticipation in returning to the farmstead.

"Can you walk or should I carry you?" he asked, a hint of laughter lacing his voice.

She lifted her head and looked at him. His hair was mussed, and she attempted to straighten it, certain she must have caused the disheveled appearance, vaguely recalling running her fingers through the silky strands.

"Don't count me out yet," she said with a weak, if teasing, grin. "I've got big plans for you."

He laughed, the sound rich and bold as he swept her into his arms and headed toward the car. "Babe," he said, planting a quick kiss on her already swollen lips. "I'm counting on it."

Chapter Ten

Traces of mauve light crept into the intimate sanctuary of the master bedroom, quietly heralding the beginning of a new day. The song from early-rising birds mingled with the rustle of leaves in the cottonwoods. The crowing of a distant rooster from a neighboring farm added to the cacophony, confirming the arrival of dawn. A gentle breeze blew through the open windows, and before long, the rest of the world would encroach upon their time together. Sam resented the hell out of that sunlight stealing into the room.

He stretched, feeling refreshed even though he'd only managed a few hours sleep during the very long, sensual night he'd spent making love to Rebecca. He flipped onto his side, crooked his elbow and rested his head in his hand, content to watch the woman he held completely responsible for his lack of shut-eye. Considering their circumstances, there were natural opponents. When they came together during the night, they were natural partners, giving in to the intensity of heat and desire, of taking and giving the ultimate pleasure.

His body stirred, confirming what his mind had a difficult time accepting: that he simply couldn't get enough of Rebecca Martinson. Regardless of their differences, making love was one area where they were perfectly in sync. She drove him crazy and made him lose control. A slow grin eased across his mouth. Her own composure had slipped to the point where his sexy counselor-at-law hadn't objected once to any of the carnal delights he'd encouraged her to share in during the night. In fact, the sensuous woman had begged him for more, her sexual appetite competing with his own.

She stirred, turning onto her back. She lifted both of her arms over her head and seemed to sink even deeper into the fluffy pillows. He didn't hesitate to take advantage, and leaned over her, nuzzling her exposed neck. Using his teeth and tongue, he brought her to full wakefulness.

She sighed and snuggled closer, wreathing her arms around his neck. "Good morning," she murmured, her voice a husky whisper.

"It will be," he promised, smiling when her satiny leg slipped between his in response.

He trailed little biting kisses down her throat and along her jaw while testing the weight of her breasts in his palm. They felt heavy and hot, and his own body's response was full and instant. Using his thumb, he teased her nipples until the dusky peaks hardened into tight buds waiting for his mouth.

She sighed and closed her eyes, her delicate hands traveling over the length of his back. With his teeth he nipped at her swollen lower lip, then soothed the spot with the tip of his tongue before taking her mouth in a hot, deep kiss. He tasted her, loved her with his mouth and felt the laziness of morning slip away as a slow-building, sensual fire sparked, ignited and gained momentum.

Keeping their lips joined, he pulled her beneath him and settled between her legs, the ridge of his arousal wedged intimately against her soft, moist curls. She rocked her hips and muttered something about forever against his mouth. Thoughts would come later. Right now he had a hot and willing woman arching her hips against him in sexual demand, making him crazy and making it impossible for him to think of anything except pleasuring her.

Rebecca gasped when Sam's mouth left hers to suckle her breast. He teased, he laved, until desire crashed through her, shattering what little defenses she had left. She was more than naked; she was exposed, heart, body and soul. He held more than her breast in his hand, he held her heart.

He shifted, the weight of his body sliding down the length of hers, his tongue creating a fire inside her only he could extinguish. Only she knew he would take his sweet time, teasing her oh, so close to the edge, only to hold the earth-shattering climax just out of her reach. During the long hours of the night, he'd kept her on the brink for so long she thought she'd go mad, until he finally brought her to heart-stopping release only to fan the flames again and again until she thought she could go no more, only to have him take her higher again.

He ignited the embers into a hot, burning flame, fanning them with his tongue, making her feel vulnerable and defenseless against his own special brand of sexual power. She didn't protest when he used his fingers and his mouth in the most intimate way a man could pleasure a woman. She twisted her hands in the sheets and sobbed as the tiny tremors shook her. He took each small tremor, delaying her release until she couldn't breathe, until she cried his name and was nothing but a mass of sensation striving toward the peak of completion. Her control became nonexistent, but Sam caught it, used it, reveled in the power he held over her body before bringing her to a mind-blowing climax that shook her to the core.

Before she could gather her thoughts or calm her racing heart, he moved over her until he settled between her legs, pushing into her with one deep, hard thrust. She welcomed his body and the pure pleasure of their joining. She kissed him, tasting herself on his mouth, and clung to him, knowing that this time wouldn't be slow or gentle. No, this time their lovemaking was going to be fast and hard, demanding and consuming.

She matched her movements to his, until he cupped

her bottom in his hands, lifting her and burying himself to the hilt. Wild, desperate passion pulled at them, driving them until reality shattered and only exquisite pleasure existed. She was burning up and half-delirious with passion as her body practically vibrated from the force of their lovemaking. Their bodies met and parted with increasing urgency while Sam ruthlessly held her where he wanted as he drove himself deep inside her over and over again, each thrust pulling her closer, guiding her to the edge until she slipped over the side.

He followed her into sweet oblivion with a low growl from deep in his throat and the tensing of his body against hers. She arched against him, his name on her lips as she sobbed from the sheer pleasurable force of her release.

They lay together, chest to breast, breathing hard as their hearts pounded in perfect rhythm. He buried his face in the crook of her neck and gently kissed her throat. Their bodies still intimately joined, he rose up on his elbows and looked at her, his eyes filled with a tenderness that made her heart ache. With equal tenderness he gently brushed the moist tendrils of hair from her face and kissed her, long and slow. He kissed her like he loved her, as if she was a treasured gift he couldn't bear to lose. She returned the kiss with equal emotion, refusing to say the words that could shatter the sweet bliss of their lovemaking.

He moved off her and rolled to his side, keeping her enclosed within his warm embrace. She sighed and closed her eyes, savoring the moment for as long as it lasted, afraid to ask for more, but fearing she could live with no less. She'd given Sam more than her body in the past twenty-four hours…she'd given him her heart, whether he wanted it or not.

THE CLOCK IN THE HALL chimed the noon hour as Rebecca drummed her fingers on the counter, munching on a piece of toast and waiting for the drip coffeemaker to deliver. They'd slept for a few more hours, made love again, dozed, then made love once again in the shower before getting dressed and venturing downstairs. She should be exhausted, but felt refreshed and looked forward to the day ahead. Sam had told her that Melanie wouldn't return from her friend's house until evening, which gave them the entire day to themselves. She grinned. Judging by their activity the past twelve hours, it wasn't much of a stretch of the imagination to guess how they'd spend their day alone.

Sam sauntered into the kitchen with that loose-hipped stroll that reminded her so much of a cowboy coming in off the range. His tan chambray shirt was tucked into jeans faded to white in all the right places. The man exuded sex appeal, and she wasn't ashamed to admit just watching him made her flush and weak with desire all at the same time. His hair, still damp from the shower and combed away from his face, emphasized the lines and planes that made him so attractive.

Her heart did a little somersault beneath her breast. When had she fallen in love with Sam Winslow? How had it happened? Or was she confusing lust with matters of the heart? When it came to men, her track record spoke for itself. She'd made drastic errors of judgment, but at least she could honestly state that none of her poor choices had ever made her feel the way she felt about Sam. With Sam the words like *complete, whole* were a part of her vocabulary. With Sam she knew a part of her had been lost for years and she'd finally found what had been missing.

Oh, God, she really *had* fallen in love with him!

"What are you frowning about?" he asked, slipping his arms around her and pulling her against him.

"Just thinking of a way to occupy our time until Melanie gets home." She planted a quick kiss on his lips and kept her emotions carefully locked away. She hadn't really lied, but her feelings were too new, too fresh and raw to be shared, especially when she had no clue as to his feelings for her.

The coffeemaker completed its cycle, and she stepped out of his embrace to pour two mugs. Sam sat at the table and opened the Sunday paper. She set the mug in front of him and decided they should probably have some breakfast. Lord knew, she certainly needed to regain her strength, but more important, she desperately needed to occupy her mind with something other than the foolish, crazy, unrealistic notion of being in love with Sam Winslow.

She opened the refrigerator and peered inside.

Wilma hadn't brought dinner or supper yesterday because the workday had been cut short due to weather, so she had no leftover pork chops, ham or chicken-fried steak to reheat along with scrambled eggs for breakfast. She tapped her index finger against her lips. There was bacon and pork sausage in the deep freeze, but she didn't trust herself to attempt those, especially with Sam being so near to see her flounder. Toast and eggs wouldn't do much for a man with Sam's appetite.

She sighed. Maybe it was time to come clean. Besides, she was tired of living a lie.

She closed the fridge, walked over to Sam and took the mug from his hand and set it on the table. She shoved the newspaper out of the way and straddled him. "Kiss me," she said, wreathing her arms around his neck and kissing him before he could so much as think about protesting.

He gripped her bottom, and the heat of his hands singed her through her jeans. He urged her closer, then ran his hands up her sides, along her rib cage and finally to cup her breasts in his large, hot hands. She sighed against his mouth. His thumbs caressed her, causing her nipples to harden and pucker against her lacy bra.

She ended the kiss as quickly as she'd initiated it, before she started to lose control and they ended up making love on the kitchen table.

"What was that all about?" he asked, a silly grin

on his face while he still held the weight of her breasts in his hands.

She took a deep breath and gathered her courage. She didn't think he'd be too upset with her, but she had lied to him, in a roundabout sort of way.

"I have a confession to make," she blurted.

Sam held his breath for a second before letting it out. Slowly he lowered his hands to rest on her hips. Despite her sensual attack, she looked serious, and that made him cautious. "Babe, after the things we did last night and this morning, I don't think there's much you can't tell me."

A slight grin tugged her lips as her eyes filled with memories of their night, and morning, of passion. "I can't cook."

The relief that shot through him was so overwhelming he was momentarily speechless. From her serious expression, he'd thought she was going to tell him she wanted to exercise those parental rights she'd never relinquished. "Really?"

"Really," she said with a serious nod. "I've been paying Wilma Parker to bring the meals for your employees. I'm sorry," she added in a rush. "It was wrong and I should have told you sooner."

She looked so guilty, his heart went out to her. "Babe, I know."

Her brow wrinkled. "You do? How?"

"You forget. I've lived here all my life. Do you know how many times I've eaten in the Shelbourne

Diner? You think I wouldn't know Wilma's cooking?''

Her mouth fell open, and she gaped at him. Then she narrowed her eyes. ''I've been feeling guilty for two weeks, every time someone complimented me on a great meal.''

She tried to stand, but he held her hips, keeping her in place. Green fire lit her gaze and fired his blood. This woman was so exciting.

''That's low, Winslow.'' Her voice was filled with outrage. ''You knew and you didn't say a single word.''

''I didn't want to hurt your feelings,'' he offered in defense.

She plucked at the buttons of his shirt. Her fingers brushed against his chest, stirring his libido.

Her gaze softened, and so did her expression. ''I don't know if that's the sweetest thing anyone's ever done for me or the cruelest. Do you know what I went through to make sure it looked like I cooked all that food myself?''

''I wondered when you'd get tired of washing pots and pans you hadn't used,'' he said with a wry chuckle.

She stopped fiddling with his shirt and crossed her arms over her chest. ''But I did have you fooled, right?''

He shook his head.

''Not once?'' she asked, her tone somewhere between incredulity and a girlish pout.

"Okay, maybe the first day or two," he conceded. "Until you blew it by having the crock pot out instead of the deep fryer."

"What?"

"Babe," he kissed her, hoping to soften the blow. "You can't fry chicken in a crock pot."

She had the good sense to blush at her mistake. "Oh."

He patted her on the rump before lifting her off his lap. "Why don't I cook breakfast," he offered, and stood. If they had to eat another serving of scrambled eggs, their cholesterol would go through the roof.

She slipped her arms around his waist and pressed her breasts against his chest. "Breakfast is the least I can do. Especially after last night," she added in a sultry voice.

He kissed her and set her away from him. "I don't mind," he said, not wanting to further damage her limited domestic ego.

She crossed the kitchen to the pantry and opened the door. "Really, Sam. I want to," she said, retrieving a carton of eggs from the shelf.

He took the carton from her and set it on the counter behind him. "We've reached our cholesterol quota for the year. How about waffles or pancakes?"

Her eyes lit up with excitement. "I can do waffles." She opened the freezer. "I found these at the market. Look, all you have to do is—"

He was right behind her, relieving her of the frozen waffles and setting them back in the freezer. "Toaster waffles don't count.'' He retrieved the ingredients for pancakes from the pantry and set them on the counter.

"Soft-boiled eggs?'' she asked, a hopeful note in her voice.

He remembered her last attempt at soft-boiled eggs and suppressed a shudder. "Save it for spring and we can dye them for the Easter Bunny.''

She planted her hands on her hips, her expression one of outrage. "Winslow, are you tired of my cooking already?''

He chuckled and ran his finger down the slope of her nose. "Rebecca, it's time you face the truth. Your talents definitely lie elsewhere.''

"Then I guess I'll set the table. That, at least, I can manage.''

SAM CLOSED THE FILE he'd been reviewing and tossed it in the filing basket on the corner of the desk. The soft leather chair creaked when he leaned back to prop his boots on the edge of the desk. Rebecca lay asleep on the leather sofa, the farming industry magazine she'd been perusing left open on the floor. He checked his watch. They had a few hours until Mel returned from Leah's house, and he still hadn't broached the subject with Rebecca that hadn't been far from his mind the past twenty-four hours.

As if she sensed him watching her, she stirred, turned on her side and looked at him. Her eyes were still hazy, and she looked sexy and sleepy, a lazy half smile canting her delicious mouth. He resisted the overwhelming urge to join her on the sofa and make love to her again.

"Rebecca, we need to talk," he said instead. What he had to say was too important to be put off any longer.

She pushed her dark hair away from her face and frowned. "This sounds serious," she said, sitting upright, a note of caution in her voice.

"Family law is your expertise, right?" He waited for her to agree, then continued. "We need to correct this parental-rights issue with Mel's adoption."

She crossed her feet at the ankles. Leaning back into the soft leather, she appeared nonchalant, but he knew enough about her body language to realize her pose as tense. She watched him carefully, ready to spring if necessary. "I take it you have a plan."

He swung his legs to the floor and stood. "We have to go back into court." He circled the desk and rested his backside on the edge. "I think we can do this quietly. Mel won't have to know. I've thought about it. It's the only way."

She leaned forward and clasped her hands together, her gaze intent as she digested the information. "Are you suggesting we reopen the adoption and start from square one?"

"Exactly," he said, relieved she understood. Perhaps this wouldn't be as difficult as he'd imagined. "You never signed away your parental rights. As it stands, you could exercise those rights."

Rebecca couldn't believe what she was hearing.

Returning to court to rectify a technicality on a four-teen-year-old adoption wasn't unheard of, but their situation was different. And far more dangerous than Sam realized. How could she explain the risks to him without telling him everything? She couldn't. It was that simple, and that complicated. "I told you I won't do that. Melanie is your daughter."

His expression turned granite hard, emphasizing his determination. "I have to be sure."

She felt the first twist of pain to her heart. "You don't trust me," she said around the sudden hurt and disillusionment clogging her throat. She'd thought he cared about her. Obviously, she'd been wrong… again. Hurt didn't begin to describe the pain and betrayal she'd felt once she'd discovered the truth about Craig Fielding. Her ego, more than her heart, had been wounded when her brief marriage to Dylan McNair ended in divorce. While she didn't believe it was possible to completely recover from the incidents surrounding the past and Craig, the pain ripping through her now at Sam's distrust bordered on crushing pain.

She stood, needing to move, to do something other than sit in front of him with her heart exposed and her emotions raw.

"It's not that—"

"My word isn't good enough for you?" she demanded, the hurt caused by his lack of trust making her lash out. "After what we shared last night?"

He muttered a gritty, heartfelt oath. "Let's leave sex out of this."

"Yes, let's," she snapped, coming to stand in front of him. She glared up at him, piqued, and terrified he'd learn the truth as to why she couldn't return to court to rectify the problems surrounding his adoption of Melanie. "You got what you wanted. Or was that your plan all along, Winslow? Soften up the birth mother to get what you want—in and out of bed?"

He flinched as if she'd slapped him, and his eyes glittered dangerously. "You're blowing this out of proportion." His calm voice belied his thunderous expression.

She turned away from him and moved to the window. She stared out at the fields beyond, wrapping her arms around her middle in an effort to keep herself from falling apart. She'd do just about anything for him, but going back into court was asking for the impossible. Not from a legal standpoint, but a personal one.

She let out a shaky breath. She had to find a way to make him understand that if he insisted on correcting the technicality, he could end up losing Mel, and there wouldn't be a damn thing she, or anyone, could do to prevent that from happening. The only way was to convince him he was asking for the impossible. "I won't go back into court, Sam," she said, keeping her back to him.

"Why the hell not?" he thundered.

She turned and sat on the window ledge. His eyebrows pulled into a deep frown, and his eyes filled with a combination of exasperation and anger.

"You're going to have to trust me," she said. There was nothing else she could say...not without revealing the truth.

He shoved a hand through his hair in agitation. "I don't trust anyone that much. Not when it comes to Mel."

She cocked her head to the side. "Anyone? Or me especially?" she asked, intentionally clouding the issues.

His initial reply was blunt and mildly profane. "That's not what I'm saying. Why do you have to make this so damned difficult?"

"This isn't as clear-cut as you think." Statutes required publication and a waiting period for interested parties to step forward and object to the adoption. If the wrong person found the publication, then all hell would break loose. And if that occurred, Sam wouldn't stand a chance of keeping Melanie. "You don't know the trouble that something like this could cause."

"Then explain it to me!" he roared, his frustration obvious.

"I can't!" she returned heatedly. She crossed the room and headed for the door, hoping her actions signaled an end to the conversation.

His hand manacled her wrist, and he spun her around to face him. "Why the hell not? What are you hiding, Rebecca?'' he demanded, his voice as heated as his expression.

She closed her eyes briefly and struggled to remain calm. "Leave it alone," she warned.

His gaze was hot and intense and filled with anger. "I will not lose my daughter."

She shrugged out of his grasp. "I'm not going to do anything to hurt your relationship with Melanie. Why can't you see that I'm trying to protect you both?"

He crossed his arms over his chest and glared down at her, ignoring her plea for understanding. "You're asking for blind faith. I can't do that."

She pulled in a deep breath and let it out slowly. "I'm sorry, Sam. You don't have a choice," she said quietly.

With nothing left to say, she spun on her heel and left him standing in the center of his office, and prayed like hell that he wouldn't pursue the issue further. Because if he did, not even her father's influence could protect them this time.

Chapter Eleven

Rebecca hit the send key on Sam's computer and waited for the printer to warm up. In the two hours since their argument, she hadn't seen him but knew he was in the family room from the sounds drifting into the study from the preseason football game on the big-screen television. She'd finished packing and had booked a motel room in the city for the night to await the morning flight that would take her back to Los Angeles. Cutting her stay short was her only option now. As long as she remained in Shelbourne, her presence would be a constant reminder to Sam of the threat she posed.

And as long as she remained, he would continue to demand the truth. He had her heart, her soul, but he could never have the truth. Better to leave now than further a fifteen-year-old lie, because that's all she could ever give him.

All she had left to do was give him the document she hoped would satisfy his concern over her exercising her parental rights, and make the necessary arrangements for a ride to Minot.

She picked up the phone and dialed Wilma Parker's number. She explained she needed to get back to Los Angeles right away, using a crisis with one of her clients as an excuse for her sudden change in plans. Thankfully Wilma hadn't asked her why Sam wasn't available. Rebecca heard the questions in the other woman's voice and chose to ignore them. By the time she hung up, she had a promise from Wilma to pick her up by six o'clock.

The clock was ticking, and her time was limited. She had a little less than three hours to wait, and hoped Wilma arrived before Melanie returned home. She might be taking the coward's way out, but she didn't think she'd survive saying goodbye to her daughter for a second time in her life. For fourteen years the sound of a newborn's cry had haunted her dreams. She could now lay those dreams to rest, for they'd been replaced.

For the rest of her life her dreams, and her waking hours, would be filled with the sweet melodic sound of her daughter's voice, her laughter and the memories of their brief time together.

Shared conversations on the front porch in the early evenings, enlightening Melanie with non-revealing and obscure details of her life in Los Angeles. Answering dozens and dozens of questions from Melanie about being a lawyer, and listening with her heart in a tight, vise-like grip as Mel explained to her she was

adopted. Laughing as her daughter played briefly with
Dutch and watching in amazement how the big Labrador retriever seemed to understand his mistress's
limitations.

The hours Sam spent in the fields left her and Melanie plenty of time to get to know each other, and
she'd treasure each of those memories for the rest of
her life. Her daughter had taught her the joys of cross-
stitch while she'd shared her knowledge of literary
classics of Homer, Virgil, and Dante. Mel had shown
her to watch the storm clouds for signs of an impending tornado and she'd reciprocated by teaching
her daughter the fine art of makeup application appropriate for a young teenager.

They'd been serious, silly and sentimental together.
Like a real mother and daughter, Rebecca thought
sadly. And Mel would never know.

She bit her lip and struggled against the tears burning her eyes. The ache in her heart was overwhelming, and she hoped over time she'd find a way to ease
the pain. Though she was leaving, her heart would
forever remain in Shelbourne, North Dakota…with
Melanie, and with Sam.

She should have listened to Victor. He'd been right.
She should have expected the heartache, and a part
of her had, but only as it extended to her daughter,
not to her daughter's father. Falling in love with Sam
had been unexpected, and had happened so quickly
she hadn't had time to steel herself against those

tender emotions. Somehow, when she wasn't paying attention, he'd crept in and stolen her heart.

How could she have known? Certainly she'd been attracted to him from the moment he'd walked into her office, and she would be lying to herself if she denied being drawn to him. Falling in love with him had been unlikely. He'd been cantankerous and belligerent in the beginning, almost to the point of being unlikable. Yet, her heart had discovered something far more wonderful beneath that gruff exterior. Her heart had discovered a gentle man filled with tenderness, caring and love. A man who touched her in places no one else had ever touched, or would ever touch her again.

The printer whirred to life, bringing her out of her thoughts. She waited for the document that would guarantee Melanie's future with Sam. Reading through one last time, she fought back a sob as she dated and signed away any perceived rights to Melanie before she could change her mind.

Pull it together, Martinson.

She let out a shaky breath and shut down the computer. If only she could close down her emotions as easily as a flip of the switch. She'd never had difficulty separating herself from emotional situations until now. Realistically, she understood the differences. This was not one of her cases or a court battle for her client. She wasn't fighting for her client's right to community property or future income of a spouse. This time she wasn't arguing a parent's right to his child. This time she was fighting for her own emotional survival and hoping to come away without too many battle scars.

She stood and looked around the room one last time. The masculine furnishings, the framed photographs of Melanie on the credenza, papers piled on the desk and atop the wood filing cabinets, the scent and essence of Sam in every nook and cranny, were filed away to be taken out later and explored. She'd treasure every single moment spent in this house, and hoped the memories were enough to last her a lifetime.

They'll have to be, she thought, turning off the desk lamp. Because in a few hours they were all she'd have to carry with her the rest of her life.

She closed the door to the office and walked purposely down the hall and into the family room. Sam sat on the edge of the sofa, his elbows resting on his knees, his hands clasped in front of him as he stared down at the carpet between his booted feet. He looked as miserable as she felt. She yearned to hold him and reassure him that he'd never lose his daughter. He was fiercely protective of Melanie, which was one of the things she loved about him. The irony of the situation wasn't lost on her. In protecting his daughter, he was doing so from the one person that loved her as much as he did—herself.

"Sam?"

He looked up at her, and her heart twisted at the pain in his eyes. She had to find a way to make him understand she would never do anything to risk his relationship with Melanie, that she wasn't betraying him by refusing to reopen the adoption to repair the existence of a technicality. She would go to the ends of the earth and back to ensure father and daughter were never separated.

She moved to the sofa and sat beside him. His scent wrapped around her, and she nearly weakened in her resolve to leave before her presence caused further damage. Yet to be so close and not touch him was pure torture. The truth was, she simply didn't trust herself not to throw her arms around him and hold on for dear life. She pulled in a deep breath and strengthened her resolve.

"Hopefully this will set your mind at ease," she said, holding the document out to him.

He didn't take it, but looked at her, his gaze full of questions, temporarily masking the pain she'd detected moments ago.

"It says I relinquish all rights, perceived and real, to any claim I may or may not have to Melanie. It's the best I can do."

He remained silent, but finally took the paper from her and scanned the contents. He shook his head and tossed the document on the cocktail table with a sound of disgust. When he turned back to face her, the anger hardening his expression was unmistakable. "I want to know one thing," he said, his voice filled with frustration. "Who are you *really* protecting? Is it your father?"

She blanched at his harshly spoken words. In protecting Sam and Melanie, yes, she was in a sense protecting her father, as well. How could she explain her relationship with her father in terms that he could understand? She couldn't, and perhaps it was better that way. "Sam, don't."

"No," he said forcefully. "I want to know. I have a right to know."

She shot off the sofa, skirted around the cocktail table and strove for calm. She wasn't going to argue with him any longer. She didn't want their last moments together to be spent in a heated discussion over something neither one of them could control.

She walked to the window and took in the wide-open space of the prairie she'd never dreamed she would ever think of calling home. If things had been different, perhaps she could have made a life here for herself, close to her daughter. Her position at Denison, Ross & Furnari was unimportant. She could walk away from her career and have no regrets, if it meant being able to spend the rest of her life with Sam. Shelbourne didn't have a lawyer and perhaps she could've opened up her own general practice. She might never get rich being a small-town attorney, but she'd gladly give away every single dime she'd earned as a junior partner, along with that in her trust fund, if it meant being a part of Melanie and Sam's life.

She sensed his nearness before he even touched her. It took every ounce of willpower she possessed not to lean into his strength. But she'd never been a wilting daisy and she wasn't about to start now. She was leaving, going back to the life she'd carved out for herself, minus her heart.

Gently he rested his hands on her shoulders and turned her around to face him. "He doesn't deserve your loyalty, Rebecca. Not after what he did to you." The tenderness in his eyes matched that of his voice, and her heart started to crumble.

She closed her eyes against the tears threatening to fall. "Please," she said, afraid to trust her voice to anything stronger than a whisper. "Please, don't do this. It doesn't matter."

"It *does* matter," he said, a note of desperation to his voice. "You've been telling me all along you didn't have a choice, and I didn't believe you. I'm deeply sorry for that. What your father did to you was wrong. You should have had a choice. That was your right. And I shouldn't be asking you to give away those rights now. It makes me no better than your father."

"Oh, Sam," she cried, around the tears clogging her throat. She reached up and cupped his warm cheek in her palm. She loved this man with all her heart, and she couldn't bear to see him hurting with self-recriminations. He'd done what a parent was supposed to do: protect his child. And now she was doing the same.

"No," she told him, hating the unsteady quality of her voice but helpless to prevent it. "That's the far-

thest thing from the truth. Melanie belongs with you.
You've been there for her all her life. You're her
father.''

"That doesn't excuse what happened to you. When
I think about how frightened you must have been,
how alone..."

"Don't do this," she pleaded. "We can't change
the past, Sam. We can only do what's necessary to
protect the future."

Sliding his hands from her shoulders to her upper
arms, he held her tight, so tight she could feel the
anger and frustration emanating from him. "Who are
you protecting?" he asked again.

She pushed away from him. "You! Why can't you
believe me? I'm protecting you and Melanie."

Sam bit back an oath and shoved his hands through
his hair in frustration. He didn't doubt Rebecca
thought she was protecting Mel, but instinct told him
there was more. Like *who* was she protecting Mel
from?

He stared at the television screen, lost in thought.
With sudden clarity he saw the truth he'd been too
blind to realize until now. While he'd been preoccu-
pied trying to protect Mel from learning the truth
about Rebecca, or worrying that she'd want to assume
a place in Mel's life, he'd missed something vitally
important. Rebecca had *never* expressed a desire to
resume her legal place in Mel's life, or even her right-
ful place. Instead, she continually insisted he was
Mel's father, all along maintaining the one secret she

felt could endanger his and Mel's life together—the true identify of Mel's biological father.

He called himself ten times a fool for not seeing the truth sooner. Sure, the two of them had become friends, and he'd even been jealous of the camaraderie between mother and daughter, but Rebecca had never encouraged anything beyond a developing friendship. She'd promised him that Mel would never know she was her birth mother, and she'd kept that promise.

He glanced at the table and the document she'd given him. Was he a fool not to trust her? Since that first moment in her office more than two weeks ago, he'd been prepared for the worst, but she'd kept her word.

Her sharp intake of breath caught his attention. He watched as she sank to the sofa as if her legs wouldn't hold her. Reaching for the remote control, her hands trembled.

Confused by her reaction, he watched her press the buttons on the remote. The volume on the television rose.

He took the remote from her and turned the volume down to a less-deafening decibel level. A news brief on the upcoming senatorial race flashed across the screen, and the color slowly drained from Rebecca's face. The newscaster highlighted the day's activities of the two high-profile candidates from California while clips rolled of the two men on the campaign trail. He finished the sixty-second spot by advising viewers to tune in later for an update on a devastating earthquake in South America following the game.

Sam looked back at Rebecca. She was trembling and her eyes were filled with stark fear. He dropped the remote on the recliner, as the truth registered. The pieces fell slowly into place; her background, her father's influential friends, and suddenly he knew. The "Craig" of her past was Craig Fielding, the deceased son of Senator Paul Fielding. Fielding used his son's untimely death caused by a drunk driver to further his own political cause, and it was common knowledge Fielding planned to make a bid for the White House in the next presidential election.

"It's him, isn't it?" he asked, already knowing the answer.

Her eyes widened, but she wouldn't look at him. "No!" She shot off the sofa and started to pace.

He stopped her mid stride and gripped her shoulders. "Don't lie to me, Rebecca. Not now. Not about this."

She tried to shrug off his grasp, but he held her tight. "Leave it alone," she cried, but he had no intention of ignoring her plea. They'd come too far now.

"Craig is Craig Fielding," he said, suspecting the truth. "Craig Fielding, the son of *Senator* Fielding, who died about ten years ago in a car accident. He's the Craig who forced himself on you in the rose garden the night Mel was conceived, isn't he? Mel's biological grandfather could be the next president of the United States.''

She closed her eyes as if the truth brought her physical pain. ''Yes,'' she whispered.

He absorbed the impact of her admission and still came up short in attempting to decipher her fears. The birth certificate the investigator unearthed indicated ''father unknown.'' Unless Rebecca was willing to name Craig Fielding as the biological father of her child, he just didn't see the risk. So what if Mel's lineage followed a path straight to the White House? He still didn't see how that could affect his relationship with Mel.

Her color had yet to return, so he guided her to the recliner and urged her to sit. She did so without argument, still refusing to look at him. There was a haunted expression in her eyes that frightened him. Almost as if there was nothing left of her but a shell.

''Don't move,'' he told her, and turned to leave. He stopped, picked up the remote control and turned off the television. They'd had enough of a shock for one afternoon, and he was having serious doubts of Rebecca's ability to handle another one. Although he was the one who should be reeling, not her, which puzzled him and made him suspect there was more here than what he'd managed to piece together so far.

He returned a few moments later with a half tumbler of whisky and pressed it into her hand. ''Drink,'' he ordered gently. She looked at him, then back at the glass in her hand.

She shook her head. "No. I'm fine," she said, setting the glass on the cocktail table.

She didn't sound or look fine to him. She looked as if she'd seen a ghost. And perhaps in a way she had, he thought. The ghosts of her past.

He crouched in front of her and clasped her hands between his. Her fingers were ice cold, and her hands still trembled. "I need to understand, Rebecca," he said, as if he was talking to a small, frightened child. "Help me understand how going into court to correct the technicality could cause me to lose Mel."

Slowly she turned her hand and laced her fingers with his. With her free hand she lightly traced the outline of his palm. "Paul Fielding has always used family values as his campaign platform," she said quietly, not looking at him.

"I don't understand."

She pulled in a deep breath and let it out slowly. When she finally looked at him, the fear had ebbed, replaced with resignation. "All adoptions must be publicized. A petition for adoption runs in the newspapers for a certain period of time, which allows anyone related to the child to object to the adoption."

He shrugged, still not understanding. "But Craig's dead."

"His father isn't. And since Senator Fielding knows about Mel, you can be sure that his closest aides have been privy to the information. Fourteen years is a long time in politics. Some of those aides may be in the other camp by now."

He gave her hand a squeeze. "Babe, that doesn't mean that I'm in danger of losing my daughter."

"Yes, Sam. It could," she said, a note of sadness lacing her voice. "It's highly probable that more than one person knew about the baby, and if any of those 'in the know' found out that a possible president's illegitimate granddaughter was up for adoption, they would see it as a golden political opportunity to discredit him. They wouldn't think twice about using Mel. I won't allow that to happen."

Understanding dawned with a slam to his gut. Anger churned inside him that anyone would dare harm his daughter for their own political gains.

"So to garner public sympathy, Fielding wouldn't hesitate to paint you and your father in a bad light. Craig's dead. It'd be your word against the memory of the senator's dead son."

"I know Fielding, Sam. He could easily object to the adoption of his biological granddaughter."

"You're saying Fielding would use Melanie as a political pawn in supporting his family values platform, and the Fielding family's right to one of their own?"

"Exactly," she said. "They wouldn't care about Melanie. All they'd be interested in is their own agenda. My father's career would be ruined. And you wouldn't stand a chance against them."

He scrubbed his hand roughly down his face, digesting everything Rebecca was telling him. He didn't give a damn about Justice Martinson's career but kept that thought to himself. Regardless of her father's treatment of her, Rebecca respected and maybe even loved him. Sam admired her loyalty, even if he did feel it was sorely misplaced.

"I'm no pauper," he said after a moment. "I would give those bastards the fight of their life if they tried to take Mel away from me."

"I know you would, but what would happen to Melanie in the meantime? The court could make her a ward of the state and you'd lose her. I can't let that happen."

She reached across the table and retrieved the document she'd given him earlier. "Take this," she said, shoving it into his hands. "It says I have no claims to Mel. No one ever needs to know the truth."

Rebecca stood and moved away from Sam. She stared at the blank television screen. The truth was out now and there was nothing she could do except pray Sam understood and would not force the technical issues of the adoption. Melanie belonged with Sam. Period. As much as she wished she could be a part of her daughter's life, she knew it would never be so.

"What are the chances of Fielding discovering Mel?" he asked.

Rebecca spun around to face him, anger and frustration tearing through her. "Dammit, why won't you let it drop? I told you I won't go back to court and I mean it, Sam. I refuse to see the two of you torn apart."

"What are the chances?" he demanded in an equally heated tone.

"None, unless you insist on reopening the adoption." She took a deep breath in an effort to calm her racing heart. "Fielding isn't going to dig anything up unless he's forced into a damage-control situation."

At his brusque nod, she crossed the short distance separating them until she stood in front of him. "Sam," she said carefully, "I know what it's like to grow up in a family that merely coexists, where appearances mean more than the emotional needs of a child. Do you think I want that kind of life for my daughter? I might not have had a choice when it came to keeping Melanie, but I do now. I'm choosing for her to stay with the man who loves her and who will protect her and never, ever put his own selfish needs above hers."

She stopped her tirade and pulled in a shaky breath. "I'm choosing, this time," she said, striving for a level tone. "It's my decision. I want my daughter to stay with you."

Sam closed his eyes and pulled her against him. She didn't hesitate, but wrapped her arms around his waist and laid her head against his chest, finding comfort in the strong arms that held her close.

"I'm sorry," he whispered against her hair. "I won't ask you again."

She pulled in a shaky breath, grateful that she'd finally gotten through to him, because she couldn't bear it if Melanie was hurt. She'd risk her own life before she'd let the Fieldings anywhere near her daughter. A parent was supposed to want better for their children, and she knew deep in her heart that she was leaving her daughter with the best possible future…with Sam.

Her insides twisted at the reminder she was leaving. Reluctantly she stepped out of his arms and looked to the clock on the wall. Wilma would be arriving within the next two hours to take her to Minot.

She turned back around, the words with her final goodbye hovering on her lips when a movement caught her attention.

She turned…and faced her daughter.

Melanie stood with her back against the wall, her arms wrapped tightly around her middle while tears streaked down her face. Pain and disillusionment filled her green eyes. What little that was left of Rebecca's heart shattered into a million pieces.

Melanie wiped at the tears running down her face. "You're my mother," she said, her tone hostile and accusatory.

Rebecca couldn't move. Couldn't speak. The one thing she'd been trying so valiantly to prevent had occurred. Melanie had been hurt, and she was to blame.

Sam moved first.

Melanie stepped away when he reached for her.

"Mel," he called, the pain in his voice matching the agony etched on his handsome face.

Melanie lifted her hand as if she didn't want to hear what Sam had to say.

"You're my mother and you didn't tell me," she accused, her eyes shooting daggers at Rebecca.

Oh, God, what could she say? All the promises she'd made, her strident arguments about protecting Mel and what had she done? Exactly what she swore she wouldn't—she'd hurt her daughter.

"I couldn't," Rebecca managed when she found her voice. "I promised—"

"You lied to me," Mel said vehemently. She cast her gaze to Sam, her hurt at his part in their betrayal evident by the pained expression on her pretty face. "You lied to me," she repeated to her father in a heated whisper.

Sam winced. "Mel, you..."

She didn't stay around to listen to their excuses or trite words of explanation, but bolted from the room instead. Moments later they heard the slamming of her bedroom door.

The sound was like a fatal blow to Rebecca's heart.

Chapter Twelve

Convinced her legs would no longer hold her, Rebecca sank onto the sofa. None of this was supposed to happen. She wasn't supposed to fall in love with Sam. No one was supposed to find out that Melanie's adoption might or might not be legal. And Melanie was definitely not supposed to learn her birth mother had come for a visit.

Dear Lord, what have we done?

She chanced a quick look over her shoulder at Sam. He stood with one hand braced against the doorjamb, the other on his hip, lost in his own thoughts. Any moment now she expected him to turn and cast the first stone, laying the blame at her feet. He'd warned her, and she'd ignored his warnings, thinking only of her own selfish need to spend time with her child. She deserved every accusation he would throw at her, but none could be any more painful than the hurtful expression on Melanie's face. That was something that would remain with Rebecca for the rest of her life, and she had no one to blame but herself.

He pushed off the wall and walked toward her. She held her breath, waiting for the words that would shatter what remained of her composure. He stopped and extended his hand. "Come on," he said, his eyes filled with determination. "We need to talk to her."

She expected recriminations, accusations, not a joint effort to soothe the girl they both loved. She shook her head. "Sam, I'm not a parent. I don't know the first thing about handling a situation like this."

He dropped his hand to his side. "You tell her the truth, and make damn sure she understands that no matter what happens, no matter how angry she is with you that you love her."

Rebecca shook her head again. How could she? She didn't have the first clue what to say. What if she said or did the wrong thing? In her career she argued tough cases before some of the most adversarial judges in the legal system. She faced the opposition and argued points of law with clear, succinct reasoning and rarely felt an ounce of fear. Even the thought of facing her father's wrath failed to produce the cold, clammy feeling creeping over her now at having to face her daughter.

"I can't," she whispered.

He stared at her in silence, for all of two seconds, before the frown fell into place. "What the hell do you mean 'you can't'? She knows who you are now. As much as we didn't want this to happen, it has, and Mel deserves an explanation."

She didn't doubt him, but the knowledge did little

to alleviate her fears. "What if I say the wrong thing?"

"You won't," he said with more confidence than she felt.

Reluctantly she stood and gathered her courage. He was right, she had to talk to Melanie. She'd answer Melanie's questions and hopefully attempt to right the wrong her coming here had caused. She'd brazenly tempted fate, and her daughter was paying the price.

"I hope you're right," she muttered, before striding past him, determined to do the right thing no matter what it cost her this time.

She climbed the steps to the upper level and walked slowly down the hall with Sam by her side. As she lifted her hand to knock on Melanie's closed door, he stopped her. "She's going to be angry. She'll ask us some tough questions," he said in a low voice. "Whatever you do, Rebecca, don't lie to her."

She nodded, shored up her courage one last time and knocked on the closed door.

"Go away."

Rebecca winced at the sound of her daughter's tear-filled voice. "Melanie? It's me. Can I come in?"

"Why? So you can lie to me some more?"

She closed her eyes and rested her head against the door separating them. Not even Sam's hand resting on her shoulder gave her comfort. Had her own parents ever felt this helpless? She didn't think so. Her father's method of parenting was a "damn the torpedoes, full steam ahead" approach. Parenting may be totally foreign to her, but she knew one thing for certain, she would never practice her father's methods.

"Mel? Please?"

"Mel, let us in," Sam said, his firm voice filled with calm reasoning.

Rebecca heard the squeak of bedsprings seconds before the door swung open. Melanie stalked across the room and dropped onto the padded window seat amid an array of stuffed toys, pulling her knees up to her chest and wrapping her slim arms around her coltish legs.

She reminded Rebecca of any number of teenage girls. The difference was *this* teenager was her very own daughter. Jeans ripped at the knee, baggy T-shirt borrowed from her father's wardrobe and long silky hair pulled into a ponytail. Typical. Everyday. She should be doing everyday, typical teenage activities like blaring her stereo or chattering on the telephone with her best friend. She shouldn't be a young girl who just had her world turned upside down by the people that loved her the most.

Rebecca quietly crossed the room to the window seat and sat beside Melanie. The girl wouldn't look at her, instead keeping her tear-filled gaze locked on the delicate peach sheers fluttering on the cool afternoon breeze.

Sam moved a pile of clothes from a bentwood rocking chair to the patchwork quilt on the bed, then sat in the rocker. He braced his elbows on his knees and clasped his hands together, his expression intent.

"Mel?" He waited until she turned her attention to him. "You're right. I wasn't honest with you and I'm sorry."

Melanie sniffled and swiped at the fresh tears brightening her eyes. Her lips quivered as she bravely attempted to keep her emotions at bay. "I can't believe you didn't tell me."

Rebecca sighed deeply. She'd give anything to take away the pain she'd caused her daughter. She'd known the risks to her own heart when she had practically blackmailed Sam to let her spend some time with Melanie, but she'd selfishly viewed the risks only as they'd applied to herself. Never once had she imagined that Melanie would learn the truth and be hurt. For that reason, she regretted ever stepping foot in North Dakota.

She reached across the small space separating them and rested her hand over her daughter's in what she hoped was a comforting gesture. Melanie stiffened but didn't pull away, which Rebecca took as encouraging.

"This isn't your dad's fault," Rebecca said when Melanie cast her teary gaze in her direction. "He didn't even want me to come here, but I insisted. I wanted to meet you."

Melanie cocked her head to the side and studied Rebecca. "Did you always know where I was?" she asked cautiously.

"No," she answered truthfully. "Not until your dad came to my office a couple of weeks ago."

"Rebecca was your donor," Sam said. "It was her bone marrow that saved your life."

Melanie listened as Sam carefully explained the details surrounding Rebecca's arrival in North Dakota, from his petitioning the court for her name to the investigator he'd hired to locate her, leaving out the all-important "blackmail" details, for which Rebecca was silently grateful.

"It's true," he said. He stood and walked slowly toward the two of them. "I didn't want Rebecca to come here. I should have told you who she was, but I didn't want you to get hurt."

He reached forward and gently cupped Melanie's cheek in his palm. Using the pad of his thumb, he wiped at a stray tear. "I was afraid I could lose you if you knew Rebecca was really your mother."

"Lose me?" Melanie's long legs unfolded and she faced her father. She eased her lithe arms tight around his middle, rested her cheek against his chest. "No way, Dad," she said in a tear-strained voice. "I love you."

Sam closed his eyes and enfolded Melanie in a loving embrace. "I love you, too, Mel," he said, his voice suspiciously tight.

Rebecca lifted a trembling hand to her lips in an effort to hold back the sob hovering in her throat. She couldn't cry. If she started, she feared she'd never stop.

After a few moments Melanie pulled away from her father and turned. Rebecca looked at her daughter, and for the first time in her life knew what it was to be a parent, to want to see your child happy and never hurting. The tears she'd tried so hard to hold back spilled forward, and a sob tore from her throat.

Melanie slipped into her arms, and Rebecca held on for dear life, unable to stop the tears, or the renewed pain caused by years of heartache over losing her only child. She cried now, for all the time she'd missed watching this beautiful child grow from an infant into the young woman she was today. Together they sat on the window seat, holding each other, unsure who was comforting whom, as they cried over the cruel hand that fate had dealt in separating a mother from her child.

Once their tears were spent, Rebecca straightened, noticing that Sam was missing. Just like a man, she thought with a wry grin, to bolt at the first sign of a woman's tears.

She smoothed Melanie's hair and gently wiped the tears from her face with a tissue from a nearby dispenser. "I've always dreamed of doing this."

Mel grinned. "What? Crying?"

"No," Rebecca chuckled. "Drying your tears. Sometimes, when I can't sleep, I'll lie in bed at night and try to imagine what you looked like. I play all sorts of little scenarios in my head. One of them was of a little girl with a skinned knee who'd asked me to kiss it and make it better. And I would, then I'd dry her tears and she'd run off happy and smiling.''

''That's so corny.''

Rebecca sighed. ''I know.''

Melanie's answering grin wavered, and she cast her gaze out the window. Rebecca sensed the shifting mood. When Melanie looked back at her, her eyes were filled with questions. ''Why did you give me away?'' she asked.

Rebecca expected this, and more, and knew the answers would be as difficult as the questions. Over the years she'd rehearsed a variety of replies, but none seemed appropriate now, only the truth would suffice at this juncture.

Grasping both of Melanie's hands in her own, she explained as carefully and honestly as possible the events surrounding the adoption. Melanie listened with rapt attention as she conveyed the truth about her lineage, pausing only when Melanie had a question or requested a deeper explanation of a certain event. When Melanie questioned her about the argument she'd overheard earlier, Rebecca hesitated for a moment, unsure how much Melanie should know regarding the technical aspects of the adoption, but opted for the truth in the end.

By the time she finished, Sam returned. He stood in the doorway, his shoulder propped against the doorjamb, his arms crossed over his chest. The look he gave her was filled with tenderness and longing. She wanted nothing more than to walk into his arms and allow the past few hours to slip away, but a quick glance at the bedside clock told her that little fantasy was impossible. Wilma would be arriving shortly. At the most, she had less than twenty minutes left before she would leave.

Melanie scooted back and leaned against the wall, crossing her legs Indian-style. Plucking one of the stuffed animals from the pile, she plopped a gray dog into her lap and fiddled with its floppy, velvet ears. "So does this mean you're going to stay here? I mean, now that I know who you are, it kinda makes sense."

The bands around Rebecca's heart tightened at the hopeful expression on Melanie's face. As much as she wished otherwise, the truth remained that her life was elsewhere. A parent was supposed to want the best for their child, and her leaving was the best thing she could do for Melanie. If she stayed, she'd only confuse the girl. Sam was her father. He was the parent here. Not her, and that truth hurt like hell.

Sadly, she shook her head. "I'm sorry. I can't stay."

Sam pushed away from the door and stepped into the room. "We'll talk about that later," he said, giving Rebecca a hard-edged glare.

Rebecca looked down at the floor, then up at Sam. "I've already called Wilma Parker," she told him. "I'm leaving tonight. I'm booked on the first plane out of Minot in the morning."

Melanie gasped. ''But you can't leave,'' she cried. ''Not now.''

''I don't belong here,'' Rebecca said, hating that her voice was shaking.

Melanie shot off the window seat and tugged on her father's hand. ''Dad, make her stay. You *have* to make her stay.''

The pleading note in Melanie's voice ripped at Rebecca's insides. Oh, God, how she hurt. A crushing weight settled on her chest, and she ached physically. She knew leaving would be difficult, she just hadn't expected it to tear her apart like this.

Rebecca stood, searching for the strength that always carried her through difficult times. ''It's best for you and your dad if I leave.''

''No!'' Melanie flung herself at her. Rebecca wrapped her arms around Mel and held tight, knowing this would be her last chance to ever hold her child in her arms. ''I just found you and now you're leaving. It's not fair.''

She looked over the top of Melanie's dark head to Sam. The heated expression flashing in his chocolate eyes had nothing to do with passion, but everything to do with anger. His fury sliced through her. She didn't have to be a mind reader to know he blamed her for Melanie's pain and confusion. She'd made a promise and she'd broken that promise. Despite her claims to the contrary, Melanie now knew she was her birth mother.

She gripped her daughter's shoulders and set her from her. "I have to, Melanie. I'm sorry."

"Can I call you? Will you visit me?"

"You can call me anytime," Rebecca answered, despite the tension radiating from Sam.

Sam pulled Melanie to his side. The action spoke volumes. He was staking his claim to what was rightfully his—his daughter. "We'll work something out," he told Melanie. "Why don't you give Rebecca and me a few minutes alone."

"Make her stay, Dad. Okay?" Melanie pleaded.

He gave his daughter a reassuring squeeze, then manacled Rebecca's wrist and pulled her from the room, down the hall and into his bedroom. He pushed the door closed, then backed her up against the wall, surrounding her with his firm, lean body. Her breath caught at the raw emotion and fury in his chilling glare.

She didn't want his anger. She wanted his lips to claim hers in a kiss that would have her toes curling and her insides melting. She wanted to slip her arms around his neck and lean into him, to feel his body pressed seductively against hers. She wanted to return his kiss with equal passion. Despite the coldness in his eyes, a sliver of hot need rose within her, sharpening the bittersweet ache in her soul.

"I warned you, Rebecca," he said, his voice tight with emotion. "Don't think you're going to be playing 'Mommy' again anytime soon."

She blanched at his harshly spoken words. He was

furious with her, and she didn't think he'd ever forgive her for hurting Melanie.

"I'm sorry," she whispered. "I never wanted this to happen."

He stepped away from her, as if he couldn't stand to be near her. "Make no mistake," he said, heatedly. "You won't see *my* daughter again."

"Sam. Please."

"Please what?"

"I don't want to leave like this. What about—" *What about the night we spent together?* She knew he cared for her. He had to. She couldn't have been wrong—again.

"Us?" He asked as if he could read her thoughts. He laughed, the cold and ruthless sound piercing her heart. "This is no *us,* Counselor. Why don't you just chalk it up to another one-night stand."

The blare of a horn intruded. "That's Wilma," she said, wanting to forget the pain and press her lips to his for one last, brief kiss. "I have to go."

He remained silent, but the hard look in his eyes was unmistakable—he'd never forgive her. And she couldn't really blame him.

The horn blared again. She waited a heartbeat, hoping Sam would give her an inkling of hope.

"Goodbye," he said coldly.

The simple word tore through her, battering her already-tattered heart. "I'm sorry," she said, her voice catching.

Calling forth every ounce of willpower she possessed, she flung open the door and hurried down the hall to the guest room. Without pause, she slung her purse and overnight bag over her shoulder, then grabbed the handle of her suitcase. Keep moving, she told herself firmly. Just keep moving.

By the time she reached the bottom of the staircase, the tears had begun to flow again. After her crying fit earlier, she wouldn't have thought she had any left to shed.

She couldn't have been more wrong.

Sam stood near the door, and Rebecca hesitated for a moment, then walked purposely toward him. She stopped and looked into his sexier-than-sin eyes, cursing the tiny shivers of awareness shooting down her spine.

She closed her eyes briefly, searching for the courage to get through the next minute. She willed herself to be strong, when she really wanted to drop her bag, slip into his arms and tell him how much she loved him.

She opened her eyes and tightened her grip on her suitcase. "Goodbye, Sam," she whispered, then stepped through the door.

SAM SWORE.

He kicked the hay bales stacked against the wall of the stable and swore again, this time more viciously.

He was a fool. A stupid, damn, stubborn fool.

He should have stopped her. He should have told her how he felt about her.

He swore again, then stabbed the pitchfork into the pile of fresh straw.

She hadn't been gone twelve hours and already he felt like a vital part of himself was missing. She was the other half that made him whole. When she'd come to his hotel room, instinct told him she was trouble with a capital *T,* and he'd been right. Only thing was, he'd never expected to fall in love with Trouble.

The old saying was true. You don't know what you have until it's gone. Thanks to his foul temper, Rebecca was gone. And she'd taken a great big chunk of his heart with her.

He finished filling the stall with fresh straw, then moved on to the next. He'd been in the barn for hours, oiling tack, making minor repairs and even mucking out stalls. He couldn't sleep and needed something to do with all the frustrated energy coursing through his body. Too bad it hadn't worked, he thought crankily, jamming the pitchfork into the pile of straw.

He shoveled more straw into the empty stall, wondering if she'd ever forgive him for the hateful things he said to her. Unless he tried, he'd never know for certain. But it was too late now.

Or was it?

He leaned the pitchfork against the side of the stall and checked his watch. She'd said she was catching the first flight out in the morning.

He scrubbed his hand roughly down his face. "It

would never work,'' he muttered to himself. They came from different worlds. He'd made the mistake before of marrying a woman he had nothing in common with, and didn't exactly relish repeating history.

She's nothing like Christina, his conscience taunted.

True, he thought. Rebecca was kind, gentle and caring. She was warm and funny. And sassy. Not to mention that one of her smoldering glances could bring him to his knees.

He headed for the door. There was no other choice. He had to go after her and tell her he loved her. If she still insisted on leaving, then there was nothing he could do about it.

He left the barn as the sun peeked over the horizon, bathing the prairie in a pinkish-gold light. The first flight out of Minot left at five forty-five. If he hurried, he could catch her.

He charged into the house and took the stairs two at a time. ''Mel,'' he bellowed on his way into the bedroom for a clean shirt. She poked her head out of the door to her bedroom and looked at him as if he'd lost his mind.

''Get dressed,'' he ordered, tugging the T-shirt over his head. ''We're going to Minot.''

''The airport?'' she asked, hopeful.

''To the airport.''

REBECCA SHOWERED, dressed and applied her makeup as if on autopilot. She welcomed the blessed numbness, afraid if she allowed herself to feel she'd fall apart. Her heart was in tatters, and she was certain her chances of recovery were slim at best.

She called the desk and ordered a cab to take her to the airport, then went about gathering her things. Fifteen minutes later, the desk clerk called to tell her the cab was waiting.

The ride from the motel to the airport took less than ten minutes. She paid her fare, then hefted her bags and walked through the automatic doors of the Minot Airport. She strode past the closed gift shop and headed to the ticket counter. The sooner she returned to Los Angeles, the sooner she could start putting her life back together.

The agent checked her bags, handed her the ticket, then pointed her in the direction of the loading gate. She looked around the waiting area, hoping, yet dreading she'd find Sam and Melanie. If they were there, she knew she wouldn't have the strength to leave. With one last look around, she satisfied her curiosity, then stepped through the electronic scanner and boarded the plane.

SAM BROKE EVERY SPEED LAW in the state as he and Mel cruised down Highway 83 to the Minot Airport. They passed the air base and the last stretch of highway that would lead them to the outskirts of the city.

Sam's heart pounded heavily in his chest when the airport came into view. The plane was still there.

He checked the mirrors for any sign of a highway

patrolman or city cop, then inched the accelerator down just a little more.

"Dad, look," Mel cried, pointing to the 707.

He bit back a curse and slowed the truck, easing to the side of the road as the 707 pulled away from the terminal and began taxiing down the runway.

Together they sat quietly in the idling truck, watching the red-and-beige airplane pick up speed then lift off. They never spoke as the plane carrying Rebecca disappeared into the bright summer morning sun until it completely disappeared from view.

It's better this way, he thought. There were too many hateful words between them, too much hurt. They were too different, with too many different wants and needs. Hadn't his disastrous marriage to Christina taught him anything?

Neither Sam nor Mel spoke when he put the truck in gear, made a U-turn and headed home. It was really better this way.

Chapter Thirteen

Rebecca perched on the edge of the chintz wing chair in her bedroom, her hands fisted in her lap. Tapping her slippered toe on the ice-blue carpeting, she stared at the egg timer she'd brought in from the kitchen. At least she'd finally found a use for the darned thing.

The seconds ticked away with agonizing slowness. The waiting was killing her. Unable to remain in one place, she slipped off the chair and began pacing between the four-poster bed and the Queen Anne dresser. In less than fifteen minutes she'd have verification that her life could indeed be irrevocably altered.

With a sound somewhere between a sigh and an agonized moan, she dropped on the bed and stared at the ceiling. A small smile curved her lips.

A baby.

She was going to have a baby.

She was going to have *Sam's* baby.

She splayed her hands over her still-flat tummy. There was no doubt in her mind that she was keeping her baby this time. Raising a child on her own would be difficult, she knew, but she was more than willing to make whatever sacrifices necessary. She wasn't going to be the first single parent on the planet, and she sure as heck wouldn't be the last, either.

The only thing she wasn't sure of was whether or not to tell Sam. He had a right to know. How could she in good conscience keep the child they'd created to herself? Nor could she deny her child the right to know its father. No matter how he felt about her, she knew he'd never turn his back on their child.

She jumped at the sound of the ringing doorbell. Frowning, she stood and tied the sash of her blue silk robe before heading toward the front door. In the six weeks since her return to Los Angeles, she still hadn't given up the foolish hope that Sam would arrive on her doorstep to sweep her off her feet with a declaration of love and beg her for forgiveness. Realistically she knew better. He'd been furious with her. But that didn't stop her from hoping or being disappointed every time the phone rang or someone arrived at her door and it wasn't Sam.

She looked through the peephole, and her frown deepened at the sight of her father. Since returning home, she'd avoided his calls. She figured he'd eventually get tired of trying to reach her and wait for her to contact him. The last thing she'd ever expected was for him to make the trip from Sacramento to Los Angeles to check up on her.

She wasn't fooling herself into thinking he was actually worried about her. Oh, no. Justice Albert Martinson's only concern would be that she'd done as ordered and obediently returned home.

She opened the door and stepped back to let him into the living room of her condominium. "Good morning, Dad," she said, unable to keep the sarcasm completely out of her voice. "What brings you to L.A.?"

He stepped inside and shrugged out of his overcoat. "I was concerned," he said, glancing around the professionally decorated living room before looking back at her. "Why haven't you returned my calls?" he asked, his voice filled with customary censure.

Whether or not she considered it fair, she had serious doubts about his supposed concern, based solely on their history. She took his coat and laid it over the back of the sofa. "I've been busy with a trial." Her hands started to tremble and she dug them in the pockets of her robe. Why did her father have to choose this time to drop by unannounced? In about ten minutes the egg timer would tell her that the waiting was over and she'd have confirmation of her suspicions. This was not a moment she wanted to share with her father.

"A six-week divorce trial?" he countered skeptically.

She pulled her hands out of her pockets and crossed her arms over her chest. "I'm sure you didn't come all the way to Los Angeles to discuss my work."

His brows pulled together in a frown, something

she was so accustomed to seeing on his aged, but still-handsome face, whenever they were in the same room together longer than fifteen minutes.

He sat in one of the fan-back chairs and propped his foot over his knee, the casual pose belying the intensity in eyes remarkably like her own. Like her own and so like Melanie's.

"I told you, I was concerned," Justice Martinson said.

She shrugged her shoulders with an air of indifference she wasn't really feeling. "As you can see, I'm just fine."

He issued a weary sigh, and she was struck by the realization that her father was getting old. Oh, she'd known he was aging, but she'd never seen him as "old" until now. In her mind he was still young and strong, with hair as black as midnight, not peppered heavily with gray or his stern features creased with deep lines.

He dropped his foot to the floor and leaned forward, resting his elbows on his knees. The look on his face was filled with a weariness she'd never detected before. Or perhaps she'd simply ignored until today.

"Rebecca, why must you always make things difficult between us?"

She dropped her arms to her side and sat on the edge of the sofa. "We've both known for a long time that we don't see eye to eye on a lot of things, Dad. Thank you for coming, but I'm fine. Really."

"Your mother's worried about you."

"I'll call her," she said, standing. "Tonight."

Her father stood, stuffed his hands in his trouser pockets and crossed the room to view a new painting she'd acquired at a starving artist's auction last week. The artist had captured the beauty and serenity of the midwest so perfectly that she'd made it her mission to acquire the painting. A summer wheat field dominated the scene, but the old farmhouse in the distance, along with the thick thunderclouds rolling in across the plains reminded her so much of Shelbourne that she'd gotten involved in a bidding war and ended up paying three times what the painting was worth.

She would have paid ten times the value. To her, the memories the painting evoked were priceless.

Her father continued to eye the painting with interest. Something was on his mind and it wasn't her taste in art. Justice Martinson was never one to beat about the bush—about anything.

Damn the torpedoes, she thought, and broached the subject she knew would lead to an argument. "Aren't you going to ask about her?"

He turned to face her, his brows pulled into a frown. "Her?"

Rebecca stood just a tad straighter. "Your granddaughter," she said quietly.

He sighed, something he did all too often in her presence. "Rebecca," he said in that voice that always told her he was disappointed in her.

She heard the ding of the egg timer, and her breath

stilled. She'd give anything to be able to dart into the bathroom, to verify that she was indeed going to have Sam's baby. But she couldn't. Not until she finished with her father. Not until she made him understand his approval and her happiness were not synonymous.

"Really, Dad," she said, her voice more brittle than she would have liked. "Melanie is a beautiful young girl. She's smart and the sweetest person I've ever had the pleasure of knowing." She shoved her hands back inside the pockets of her robe again and faced him.

"She looks a little like me, and a little like Craig." She pulled in a deep breath and let it out slow in an effort to hold back the tears of frustration. "I can even see some of Mom in her, too," she added, her voice catching.

"Rebecca—"

"But you know what?" She stepped away when he moved toward her. "She's happy, Dad. And that makes me happy. But you know what else? I'm also damned grateful. She has a father who loves her, and who'll stand by her no matter what. No matter if she does disappoint him, Sam is *always* going to love her."

The pain that flashed in his eyes mirrored that in her heart. "You think I don't love you?"

She couldn't answer him. The words wouldn't move past the tears clogging her throat.

"What do you want? Do you want this child of

yours? I can do it for you. Will that make you happy?"

She dropped on the edge of the sofa and shook her head wearily. "You just don't get it," she said, finding her voice. "I don't want *you* to do anything. I'm thirty-one years old, Dad. Don't you think it's time you stopped second-guessing me and let me make my own decisions?"

"You've made your own decisions," he countered.

"And you've been right behind me criticizing me every step of the way," she returned.

He moved to the chair he'd vacated earlier and sat. When he looked at her, she no longer saw the angry father who had little patience for a curious child. Instead she saw a man in his sixties filled with regrets. "I've only wanted the best for you. Is that so wrong?"

Neither of them could change the past, nor could they correct all the mistakes they'd both made over the years. She didn't know if they'd ever be in agreement on any issue. Their roles had been cast many years before, and if she'd inherited anything from her father, it was his stubbornness. Regardless of past hurts, he was her father and she loved him.

"No, Dad, it isn't," she said quietly. He wouldn't apologize for the past, and she didn't expect him to. But she was through looking for his approval, and that was something he was going to have to accept. Until he did, they would continue to be at odds.

"There's coffee in the kitchen," she said rising.

"Help yourself while I get dressed. Since I don't have to be in court until this afternoon, I'll buy you breakfast."

Extending olive branches was never her strong suit, but this was her father and she was at least willing to try. If they couldn't correct the past, perhaps they could at least attempt to forge a better future.

He looked up at her, and the hope in his clear green eyes was encouraging. "I'd like that."

She waited until he stepped into the kitchen before hurrying into the bathroom. The home pregnancy test sat on the marble counter. With trembling fingers, she picked up the test stick.

Joy swept through her.

She was going to have a baby.

She was going to have *Sam's* baby.

Tears, happy tears, flowed down her cheeks. She made a sound, somewhere between a laugh and a cry of joy.

She was going to have a baby!

"Rebecca! Rebecca, are you all right?"

She turned at the sound of her father's voice. He stood in the threshold of her bedroom, his eyes filled with concern—something she'd rarely seen from him.

She lamely held up the test strip. "It's blue," she said through her tears.

"You're pregnant?"

She swiped at the moisture covering her cheeks and nodded, not the least offended by his shocked expression.

"Haven't you learned anything? My God, Rebecca. After what Craig did to you—"

"You have no right to judge me," she said, forcing herself to remain calm. If she and her father really were going to mend their relationship, getting into their typical shouting match would only serve to drive the wedge deeper between them. She wasn't seventeen anymore. This time he couldn't do what he insisted was best for her. This time the decision, the choices were hers to make.

Hers. And Sam's.

"As your father—"

She slapped the test strip on the dresser and planted her hands on her hips. "Then act like one and be supportive, Dad. Don't make the same mistake twice."

He spun on his heel and stormed out of her bedroom. She started after him, telling herself she should just let him go and accept the fact that they would never be close. They were both too stubborn, and as her mother once told her, too much alike.

By the time she reached the living room, she expected to find him shrugging into his coat. Instead he was seated in the chair again, his elbows propped on his knees and holding his head in his hands.

She sat on the edge of the sofa. "Dad. I'm keeping my baby. It would make me happy if you'd support my decision. If you can't, then I'm sorry, we have nothing left to say to each other."

He lifted his gaze to hers. Concern bracketed his

eyes, giving her hope that they could overcome the obstacles and at least attempt to have a better relationship. "Do you realize how difficult it's going to be raising a child on your own?"

"I know it'll be tough," she said. "But I'm keeping my baby, Dad. Don't even try to change my mind."

He stood and walked into the kitchen. She knew he was attempting to come to terms with her decision and needed a few moments alone. Curling her legs beneath her on the sofa, she waited. When he returned moments later, he carried two mugs of coffee.

"What are you going to do?" he asked, handing her one.

She wrapped her fingers around the ceramic mug. "I guess I need to call Sam. He has a right to know."

"Can I offer some advice?" he asked, taking the chair he'd vacated earlier.

At her answering nod, he said, "Go see him. Telling a man he's about to become a father isn't something you should do on the phone."

She leaned forward and carefully set her mug on the table. "No. I couldn't." How could she return after he'd practically ordered her out of his home? The hurt between them was just too painful and she didn't think she could face it all over again. Besides, just because she was carrying Sam's baby didn't add up to forgiveness, no matter how inadvertent the damage she'd caused. She'd broken her promise, and for that she knew he would never forgive her.

"What are you afraid of?" he asked, looking at her over the rim of his coffee mug.

"I'm not afraid of anything," she said, sounding like a petulant child, but unwilling to tell him she was afraid, terrified that Sam would crush her already-broken heart.

"Good," her father said, an odd light in his eyes she didn't recognize. "I'd hate to think you'd changed suddenly. You've never been afraid of anything your entire life."

She narrowed her eyes on her father at his condescending tone. "I'm not afraid," she repeated firmly.

"Then go see him."

She unfolded her legs and leaned forward, burying her face in her hands. "I can't."

"Does he return your feelings?" he asked, vocalizing what she feared more than telling Sam he was about to become a father.

In the weeks since she'd returned to Los Angeles, Melanie called her at least once a week. Rebecca called at least twice, always making certain she called when she knew Sam would be in the fields. She didn't even know if he was aware of Melanie's calls. And her own foolish and stubborn pride kept her from asking for him.

"Are you in love with him?" her father asked.

She rose from the sofa and walked over to look at the painting that reminded her so much of what she'd left behind in Shelbourne. There was no doubt in her mind about her feelings for Sam. When she'd left, her heart remained with him, whether he wanted it or not.

"I never thought it would hurt like this," she said turning to her father. "And don't ask me why I fell in love with him, because I couldn't tell you. He's cranky and stubborn," she said, planting her hands on her hips, thinking of how difficult he'd been.

"He's a wonderful father, so patient and understanding," she said, her expression softening. "His temper needs work and he can be the most obstinate man I've ever met. But he's so sweet and tender. He makes me laugh. He—"

"Rebecca?" he interrupted with an uncharacteristic chuckle. "Go to him, or you'll never know how he feels."

She wrapped her arms around her middle and looked at her father. "That's the problem. I *do* know how he feels."

"What if you're wrong," he reasoned. "Contrary to your opinion, you're not always right, Rebecca."

Her grin was wry. "What if I'm not wrong?"

Justice Martinson stood and crossed the space separating them. Gently he lifted her chin until she had no choice but to look into his eyes. She wouldn't exactly say she saw love in her father's gaze, but she did detect concern. For now that was enough. She wouldn't ask for more.

"Then you go on," he said wisely.

HER FATHER'S WORDS echoed through her mind for the rest of the morning, haunting her during the final stages of the trial when she needed to concentrate. She could think about the future later, on the flight she'd booked that would take her to North Dakota, but now her client, Peter Grant, could lose his parental rights, and she needed to focus.

Weeks of preparation, hour upon hour spent poring over discovery documents, and long hours in conference preparing her client for trial had boiled down to this final moment. She had an obligation to her client, and he couldn't afford for her to be distracted with her own problems.

Forcing herself to concentrate on the moments ahead, she waited for the petitioner's attorney to return to his seat after delivering his closing argument. The picture he painted of her client was one of a man too wrapped up in his own career to take an interest in the lives of his children, which she hoped the exhibits admitted into evidence were strong enough to overrule.

She took a deep breath and stood. "Your Honor," she started, and walked around the table. "You've seen the evidence presented by my client. We've entered the exhibits into the record consisting of telephone bills with proof of my client's numerous telephone calls made to the petitioner's residence. We've played the various recordings of the petitioner's current husband refusing to allow my client to speak to his children. The court has been provided airline ticket receipts for the trips Mr. Grant has made in an attempt to visit his children, only to be turned away by the petitioner. We've shown evidence that my client has repeatedly attempted to exercise his visitation rights as ordered by this court in the divorce. And we've also shown the petitioner's continual gross denial of my client's basic rights as a parent.''

She turned and indicated her client with a wave of her hand. ''This is not a man too busy to spend time with his children as the petitioner would have you believe. He's a man who's been denied the fundamental right of a parent to partake in the rearing of his children.''

For effect, she walked slowly toward her client's ex-wife and her current husband. She tried to make eye contact, but the former Mrs. Grant refused to look at her. ''Through no fault of his own, Mr. Grant has been prevented from participating in the everyday activities of his children. Because of the petitioner, Mr. Grant was turned away from his son's sixteenth birthday party. When he attempted to attend his twelve-year-old daughter's ballet recital, he was forcefully prevented from doing so by the petitioner's husband.''

Slipping her hands in the side pockets of her navy-blue skirt, she strolled back toward Peter Grant. She turned and propped her backside against the counsel table and faced the judge. ''My client was not given a choice,'' she said, no longer certain whether she was speaking for herself or her client.

''The decision was ripped from his hands by the

petitioner and her husband,'' she said, straightening, as a hefty dose of guilt settled on her shoulders. For as much as she claimed her own rights had been denied, she knew what she had to do. She was no better than her father if she didn't at least attempt to go to Sam and tell him that they were having a child. There was nothing she could do to right the wrongs of the past, for to do so would accomplish nothing but more pain and heartache for Melanie.

But she could do what was right this time. The choice *was* hers now.

''Mr. Grant's continual pleas to be a part of the lives of his children to the petitioner have been unilaterally denied,'' she continued. ''It is up to you, Your Honor, to allow my client to maintain what is rightfully his...his children. The adoption of my client's children by the petitioner's current husband must be denied. There is no other conscionable decision that can be made.''

By the time she returned to her chair, her legs were shaking. There was nothing else to be done, but await the judge's decision. He could make a ruling from the bench, or take the matter under advisement, which could mean a wait of thirty to sixty days.

Judge Holden removed his bifocals and looked at the parties, first the petitioner, then the respondent, Peter Grant. He cleared his throat and leaned forward, resting his arms on the bench. ''Our courts are overflowing with cases of nonsupport, or as the press has labeled them, deadbeat dads and/or moms. This case has no such allegation. Mr. Grant has faithfully paid for the support of his children for the past ten-plus years, well above the standard state guidelines.''

Rebecca breathed a quick sigh of relief as her hopes climbed a notch.

"Each month I'm asked to rule in cases of custody," the judge continued. "I've heard petitions for adoption where the biological parents have had no contact with their children for years. In all my years on the bench I have seen reprehensible acts by couples of divorce and the effect their actions have on their children. The petitioner's actions are remarkably suspect, and I have to wonder at the damage done to the minor children of the parties in this action. The petition for adoption is denied."

Rebecca laid her hand over Peter's and gave him a reassuring squeeze.

"Mr. Grant, I do not feel I would be remiss in stating that under the circumstances this court would heartily entertain a motion to amend custody."

"Thank you, Your Honor," Rebecca said, standing. "I'll confer with my client at length on the matter."

After she accepted the thanks and gratitude of her client, she exchanged a few words with opposing counsel before leaving the courthouse, one thought firmly in her mind. In a matter of hours, she'd be with Sam again—if only to tell him he was going to be a father.

As difficult as it was to accept her father's advice,

given their past history, this was one time she couldn't deny he spoke the truth. She knew in her own heart she might not have the power to right the wrongs committed fifteen years ago, but she did have the power to prevent history from repeating itself.

Or hurting Sam, she thought suddenly. Whether or not he returned her love wasn't the issue. The issue was his right to know his child. Their child. Hadn't her own experiences taught her that much?

By tomorrow this time, he would know about the child she carried. And regardless of his feelings for her, her father was right—she would go on.

Chapter Fourteen

By the time Sam pulled the rental car into the condominium complex, his nerves were stretched tight. If anyone had told him he'd be as nervous as a teenager about to ask the prettiest girl in town to the senior prom, he would have laughed in their face. Now, staring at the block of units, trying to figure out which one was 689, he wasn't so sure.

Since Rebecca walked out of his life, he'd been just downright miserable. Hell, he'd been as crabby as an old bear and about as impossible to be near. Even Mel had finally gotten fed up with him and read him the riot act. He figured if he didn't get his butt to California and convince Rebecca to forgive him for being such a bastard and come home with him where she belonged, his own daughter could end up disowning him.

He turned off the ignition and stepped from the car into the warmth of the early evening. Already in Shelbourne the temperatures were dipping into the twenties and thirties, making the ninety-plus degrees of

Los Angeles feel oppressive in comparison. He patted his pocket, checking again, for what must have been the tenth time since he'd left Shelbourne, for the blue velvet box that held the engagement ring he planned to give her and beg, if necessary, for her to accept it and him.

After wandering around the hilly complex for nearly ten minutes, he finally located Rebecca's upstairs unit which overlooked the hustle and bustle of Century City. He approached the door and before he could change his mind, rang the bell.

She opened the door seconds later, wearing a royal-blue silk robe and a fluffy white towel wrapped around her head turban-style. A classical overture played on a stereo in the background. Raw emotion played across her delicate features, catching and holding his attention. In the space of seconds he detected joy and apprehension along with a hint of fear that heightened his guilt. That apprehension and fear annoyed him, and he blamed himself. He'd spent the long flight west with self-recrimination as his traveling companion. For now he would concentrate on her first reaction. Joy. She was happy to see him, and that gave him a surge of renewed hope.

"Aren't you going to ask me in?" he said with an air of confidence he was nowhere near feeling.

"Of course," she said, swinging the door open wide. "Please. Come in."

He despised the formality in her voice, as if they were nothing more than polite strangers. After what they'd shared, he felt slightly insulted, but he couldn't blame her.

She gripped the lapels of her robe, and he couldn't help noticing the way the silk clung to her curves. His gut tightened at the erotic images that instantly flared to life through his mind.

"Is Melanie all right?" she asked, motioning him inside.

"She's fine." He looked around the room with its soft colors and subtle shades of mauve, gray and blue and was struck by the emptiness of the room. There were furnishings and other items which blended perfectly together, but there was nothing that said the room, or the things in it, belonged to Rebecca. Until he turned back to face her and he caught a glimpse of a painting so completely out of place.

His heart stopped, then resumed at a maddening pace. Behind her hung a midwestern farm scene, remarkably reminiscent of Shelbourne.

"She misses you," he said.

Her expression softened, her green eyes filling with tenderness. "I miss her, too," she said quietly, indicating for him to sit. "I think about her all the time."

He moved to the sofa and sat on the edge. "You always did, didn't you? Think about her, I mean. Even before you knew who she was."

Rebecca sat in one of the low-backed chairs, making sure her robe covered her. She was fully aware she was naked beneath the silken barrier and Sam was less than four feet away.

"Why are you here?" she asked, carefully evading his question. For as many times as she'd hoped and been disappointed that Sam hadn't come chasing after her with a declaration of love, she was too cautious to have her hopes raised by his unexpected visit. Chances were more than likely the purpose of his visit had to do with yet another demand she reopen the adoption to correct a fourteen-year-old technicality. "You didn't travel all this way just to tell me that Melanie misses me."

That deep frown she'd always associated with him fell into place. He stood, crossed to the entertainment center and flipped off her stereo, then turned to face her, his hands planted on his hips. "No, I didn't," he said grumpily.

"Then why are you here?" she asked calmly, despite the rapid cadence of her heart. She was too afraid to hope, too afraid of being disappointed yet again.

"I missed you, too," he said, his frown deepening and his voice filling with frustration. "It just hasn't been the same since you left. Hell, nothing's the same."

Her heart soared. She wanted to leap off the chair and into his arms, but restrained herself, still fearful the heavy cloud of doubt would weigh too heavily for her hopes to find the light of day.

"Half the hands are ready to quit because I've been such a bear lately."

Considering she'd seen his temper firsthand, she

could just imagine what he'd been like. Bear was putting it lightly, she thought with a smile.

"Jake's quit twice this month already and threatening to leave for good next time. Mel won't even talk to me half the time." He stopped his tirade and stared at her.

"What are you grinning about?" he groused. "I've been miserable since you left. Dammit, woman, say something."

Slowly she stood and approached him, her heart overflowing with love for this cantankerous, sexier-than-sin "plowboy," who had somehow stolen her heart when she wasn't looking. She slipped her arms around his neck and teased the hair that brushed the collar of his corduroy jacket. His eyes darkened as his hands settled on her hips and pulled her against him.

"I love you," she said, knowing the only risk she was taking was if she *didn't* tell him what was in her heart.

He sighed, as if he'd been waiting all his life to hear those words. He dipped his head and tugged on her lower lip with his teeth. "Say it again," he demanded against her lips while pulling the towel from her hair.

"I love you, Sam," she managed to say, before his lips captured hers in one of those kisses that made her insides quiver and her body come alive with desire. His hands left her hips and he sank them into her hair, holding her still while he played havoc with her senses. Need pooled deep in her belly, and her legs went weak giving her no choice but to sink into him. He caught her and held her, as she knew he would do for the rest of their lives.

He lifted his head, but refused to let her go. She had the distinct impression he would never let her go. "Do you know how much I love you?" he asked, planting little biting kisses along her jaw.

She wiggled against him. "I think I have an idea," she countered.

He reared back and cocked a brow at her sass. "Does that mean you'll marry me and make an honest man out of me?"

His teasing comment reminded her of the baby. She stepped out of his embrace, needing some distance to gather her thoughts.

"What is it?" he asked, concern etched on his face. "Are you worried about your job?"

She shook her head, searching for the right way to tell him he was going to be a father. He loved Melanie, but would he want another child? Melanie was more than half-grown. He might not want more children.

He closed the distance between them, resting his hands on her shoulders. "Hang a shingle out at the farmstead. Hell, I'll buy you a building in Shelbourne if that's what you want. If that doesn't appeal to you, then Mel and I will move here. We'll work something out. Just say you'll marry me, Rebecca. I love you. Say you'll be my wife."

An abundance of love shone in those bedroom eyes she adored and knew she would adore until she drew her last breath. The realization gave her strength. "I'll marry you. But, there's something I need to say first."

"Just tell me you'll forgive me for being a first-class jerk. I'm sorry, babe. I never meant to hurt you. I'll make it up to you if it takes the rest of my life."

She placed her fingers gently over his lips. "Shh. It isn't important."

He grasped her hand in his. "Yes, it is. I was wrong. It wasn't your fault Mel found out. Can you forgive me?"

"Yes, but Sam—"

"If it's about Mel and your rights, you can stop right there. I tore up that piece of paper you signed. Unless we do something, there's no way anyone could find out about her."

She pulled in a deep breath and let it out slowly. She looked into his eyes, those darker-than-sin bedroom eyes that had the power to melt her soul, and knew he'd always be there for her. "I'm pregnant," she said finally.

A series of emotions crossed his handsome face, none of which indicated displeasure.

"Pregnant?" he asked, his face splitting into a wide, silly grin.

She nodded. "Pregnant."

"Pregnant," he repeated, wrapping his arms around her and kissing her senseless. When he finally lifted his head, he asked, "How did that happen?"

She arched an eyebrow at him and shook her head in mock dismay. "The usual way, plowboy. In case it slipped your mind, we didn't use any birth control."

"Are you sure?" he asked, still refusing to let go of her.

"That we didn't use birth control? Positive."

"That you're pregnant."

"Oh, that. Yes, it's *positive.*"

He kissed her briefly. "Then I guess I'll really have to marry you now."

She laughed and poked him gently in the ribs. "You already asked me, Winslow."

The teasing light left his eyes, replaced by a tenderness that made her heart ache. He reached into the inside pocket of his jacket and produced a small velvet box. Carefully he opened the lid. Nestled inside was a marquee diamond surrounded with delicate emerald stones.

"I love you, Rebecca." His husky voice filled with the same emotion banked in his eyes…love. "Be my wife."

"Yes," she whispered, with tears of happiness blurring her vision.

Ten Months Later

WITH THE TOE OF HER SNEAKER Rebecca set the rocking chair into motion once again. As her infant daughter slept peacefully in her arms, she marveled once again at the changes in her life. A year ago if someone had told her she'd give up a successful career to re-locate to a small midwestern farming community and become the wife of a very successful landowner and mother of two, she'd have laughed hysterically. The truth was, since she'd traded her law books in for cookbooks, Rebecca Martinson Winslow had never been happier in her life.

"Mom, can I hold her?"

Rebecca smiled at Melanie and gently handed Samantha Winslow to her big sister. "Watch her head, honey," she said quietly so as not to awaken the sleeping infant.

Melanie rolled her eyes. "I know, Mom."

Rebecca hovered nearby until Melanie settled herself into the rocker before slipping quietly from the nursery and hurrying downstairs to the kitchen. She had a cake waiting to be frosted for the buffet table at the annual harvest dance later that night and knew that Samantha wouldn't sleep for long.

She entered the kitchen and her heart sank. The beautiful chocolate cake she'd taken out of the oven a little more than an hour ago to cool was as flat as the pancakes Sam cooked for breakfast that morning.

"Problems?" Sam asked, coming up behind her and wrapping his arms around her.

"Just another reminder that I'm a culinary disaster," she complained, laying her head back against his shoulder.

"Don't be so hard on yourself," he said, placing a

kiss on her neck. "I didn't marry you because you could cook."

"It's a good thing," she quipped. "I'd be a divorcee by now."

He chuckled and she turned in his arms, wreathed her arms around his neck and pressed her lips briefly to his. "I'll be the only wife at the dance tonight with nothing on the buffet table."

"Speaking of the dance, wear that little black thing again this year. I have…fond memories of that dress," he said, wiggling his eyebrows lasciviously.

She laughed. "You have fond memories of what happened *after* the dance," she teased, pressing her body seductively against his.

"Yeah, you did have your way with me that night."

Before she could summon a tart reply, she heard the first fussy cries of Samantha, followed by the plaintive wail of distress from her older daughter seeking assistance.

She reluctantly slipped out of her husband's warm embrace and headed upstairs. Sam followed her into the nursery and took the baby from Melanie. Samantha's cries stilled and she gurgled and cooed at her father.

Melanie made a sound of disgust and dug her hands in the back pockets of her jeans. "How do you do that?" she asked her father.

"I have a way with women," he said, running his finger down the slope of his older daughter's nose.

Rebecca leaned against the door as she watched Sam with his girls. He sat on the window seat, making nonsensical noises to the baby. Samantha cooed in his arms, and Melanie draped her arms around his neck and leaned over his shoulder, talking and cooing back at her baby sister.

Yes, he certainly did have a way with women, Rebecca thought with a dreamy smile as she lovingly watched her family. Her husband definitely had a way with her, a way that led straight to her heart.

Her years as a family law attorney had nearly destroyed her faith in the sanctity of marriage. Too often she'd seen the hurtful side of marriage, and had even suffered her own disappointments in a previous union. The day one wide-shouldered, dark-haired plowboy walked into her office, she'd learned one very valuable lesson...

There was such a thing as happily-ever-after, and she and Sam would love there together.

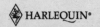

*Harlequin truly does
make any time special....
This year we are celebrating
weddings in style!*

To help us celebrate, we want you to tell us how wearing the Harlequin wedding gown will make your wedding day special. As the grand prize, Harlequin will offer one lucky bride the chance to "Walk Down the Aisle" in the Harlequin wedding gown!

There's more...

For her honeymoon, she and her groom will spend five nights at the **Hyatt Regency Maui.** As part of this five-night honeymoon at the hotel renowned for its romantic attractions, the couple will enjoy a candlelit dinner for two in Swan Court, a sunset sail on the hotel's catamaran, and duet spa treatments.

To enter, please write, in, 250 words or less, how wearing the Harlequin wedding gown will make your wedding day special. The entry will be judged based on its emotionally compelling nature, its originality and creativity, and its sincerity. This contest is open to Canadian and U.S. residents only and to those who are 18 years of age and older. There is no purchase necessary to enter. Void where prohibited. See further contest rules attached. Please send your entry to:

Walk Down the Aisle Contest

In Canada	In U.S.A.
P.O. Box 637	P.O. Box 9076
Fort Erie, Ontario	3010 Walden Ave.
L2A 5X3	Buffalo, NY 14269-9076

You can also enter by visiting www.eHarlequin.com
Win the Harlequin wedding gown and the vacation of a lifetime!
The deadline for entries is October 1, 2001.

HARLEQUIN®
Makes any time special ®

PHWDACONT1

HARLEQUIN WALK DOWN THE AISLE TO MAUI CONTEST 1197
OFFICIAL RULES
NO PURCHASE NECESSARY TO ENTER

1. To enter, follow directions published in the offer to which you are responding. Contest begins April 2, 2001, and ends on October 1, 2001. Method of entry may vary. Mailed entries must be postmarked by October 1, 2001, and received by October 8, 2001.

2. Contest entry may be, at times, presented via the Internet, but will be restricted solely to residents of certain geographic areas that are disclosed on the Web site. To enter via the Internet, if permissible, access the Harlequin Web site (www.eHarlequin.com) and follow the directions displayed online. Online entries must be received by 11:59 p.m. E.S.T. on October 1, 2001.

   In lieu of submitting an entry online, enter by mail by hand-printing (or typing) on an 8½" x 11" plain piece of paper, your name, address (including zip code), Contest number/name and in 250 words or fewer, why winning a Harlequin wedding dress would make your wedding day special. Mail via first-class mail to: Harlequin Walk Down the Aisle Contest 1197, (in the U.S.) P.O. Box 9076, 3010 Walden Avenue, Buffalo, NY 14269-9076, (in Canada) P.O. Box 637, Fort Erie, Ontario L2A 5X3, Canada. Limit one entry per person, household address and e-mail address. Online and/or mailed entries received from persons residing in geographic areas in which Internet entry is not permissible will be disqualified.

3. Contests will be judged by a panel of members of the Harlequin editorial, marketing and public relations staff based on the following criteria:

   - Originality and Creativity—50%
   - Emotionally Compelling—25%
   - Sincerity—25%

   In the event of a tie, duplicate prizes will be awarded. Decisions of the judges are final.

4. All entries become the property of Torstar Corp. and will not be returned. No responsibility is assumed for lost, late, illegible, incomplete, inaccurate, nondelivered or misdirected mail or misdirected e-mail, for technical, hardware or software failures of any kind, lost or unavailable network connections, or failed, incomplete, garbled or delayed computer transmission or any human error which may occur in the receipt or processing of the entries in this Contest.

5. Contest open only to residents of the U.S. (except Puerto Rico) and Canada, who are 18 years of age or older, and is void wherever prohibited by law; all applicable laws and regulations apply. Any litigation within the Province of Quebec respecting the conduct or organization of a publicity contest may be submitted to the Régie des alcools, des courses et des jeux for a ruling. Any litigation respecting the awarding of a prize may be submitted to the Régie des alcools, des courses et des jeux only for the purpose of helping the parties reach a settlement. Employees and immediate family members of Torstar Corp. and D. L. Blair, Inc., their affiliates, subsidiaries and all other agencies, entities and persons connected with the use, marketing or conduct of this Contest are not eligible to enter. Taxes on prizes are the sole responsibility of winners. Acceptance of any prize offered constitutes permission to use winner's name, photograph or other likeness for the purposes of advertising, trade and promotion on behalf of Torstar Corp., its affiliates and subsidiaries without further compensation to the winner, unless prohibited by law.

6. Winners will be determined no later than November 15, 2001, and will be notified by mail. Winners will be required to sign and return an Affidavit of Eligibility form within 15 days after winner notification. Noncompliance within that time period may result in disqualification and an alternative winner may be selected. Winners of trip must execute a Release of Liability prior to ticketing and must possess required travel documents (e.g. passport, photo ID) where applicable. Trip must be completed by November 2002. No substitution of prize permitted by winner. Torstar Corp. and D. L. Blair, Inc., their parents, affiliates, and subsidiaries are not responsible for errors in printing or electronic presentation of Contest, entries and/or game pieces. In the event of printing or other errors which may result in unintended prize values or duplication of prizes, all affected game pieces or entries shall be null and void. If for any reason the Internet portion of the Contest is not capable of running as planned, including infection by computer virus, bugs, tampering, unauthorized intervention, fraud, technical failures, or any other causes beyond the control of Torstar Corp. which corrupt or affect the administration, secrecy, fairness, integrity or proper conduct of the Contest, Torstar Corp. reserves the right, at its sole discretion, to disqualify any individual who tampers with the entry process and to cancel, terminate, modify or suspend the Contest or the Internet portion thereof. In the event of a dispute regarding any online entry, the entry will be deemed submitted by the authorized holder of the e-mail account submitted at the time of entry. Authorized account holder is defined as the natural person who is assigned to an e-mail address by an Internet access provider, online service provider or other organization that is responsible for arranging e-mail address for the domain associated with the submitted e-mail address. **Purchase or acceptance of a product offer does not improve your chances of winning.**

7. Prizes: (1) Grand Prize—A Harlequin wedding dress (approximate retail value: $3,500) and a 5-night/6-day honeymoon trip to Maui, HI, including round-trip air transportation provided by Maui Visitors Bureau from Los Angeles International Airport (winner is responsible for transportation to and from Los Angeles International Airport) and a Harlequin Romance Package, including hotel accomodations (double occupancy) at the Hyatt Regency Maui Resort and Spa, dinner for (2) two at Swan Court, a sunset sail on Kiele V and a spa treatment for the winner (approximate retail value: $4,000); (5) Five runner-up prizes of a $1000 gift certificate to selected retail outlets to be determined by Sponsor (retail value $1000 ea.). Prizes consist of only those items listed as part of the prize. Limit one prize per person. All prizes are valued in U.S. currency.

8. For a list of winners (available after December 17, 2001) send a self-addressed, stamped envelope to: Harlequin Walk Down the Aisle Contest 1197 Winners, P.O. Box 4200 Blair, NE 68009-4200 or you may access the www.eHarlequin.com Web site through January 15, 2002.

Contest sponsored by Torstar Corp., P.O. Box 9042, Buffalo, NY 14269-9042, U.S.A.

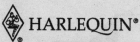

COMING SOON...

AN EXCITING
OPPORTUNITY TO SAVE
ON THE PURCHASE OF
HARLEQUIN AND
SILHOUETTE BOOKS!

*DETAILS TO FOLLOW
IN OCTOBER 2001!*

YOU WON'T WANT TO MISS IT!

PHQ401